JAN 0 4

DATE DUE

GAYLORD			PRINTED IN U.S.A.

Revenge of
the Heart

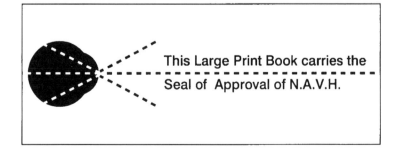

Revenge of the Heart

Barbara Cartland

Thorndike Press • **Waterville, Maine**

Copyright © 1984 by Barbara Cartland

Published in 2003 by arrangement with
International Book Marketing Limited.

Thorndike Press® Large Print Romance.

The tree indicium is a trademark of Thorndike Press.

The text of this Large Print edition is unabridged.
Other aspects of the book may vary from the original edition.

Set in 16 pt. Plantin by Al Chase.

Printed in the United States on permanent paper.

Library of Congress Cataloging-in-Publication Data

Cartland, Barbara, 1902–
    Revenge of the heart : a new Camfield novel of love /
by Barbara Cartland.
        p. cm.
    ISBN 0-7862-5897-7 (lg. print : hc : alk. paper)
    1. Triangles (Interpersonal relations) — Fiction.
2. Nobility — Fiction.   3. Revenge — Fiction.   4. Large
type books.   I. Title.
PR6005.A765R47 2003
    823′.912—dc22   2003060781

Revenge of
the Heart

As the Founder/CEO of NAVH, the only national health agency solely devoted to those who, although not totally blind, have an eye disease which could lead to serious visual impairment, I am pleased to recognize Thorndike Press* as one of the leading publishers in the large print field.

Founded in 1954 in San Francisco to prepare large print textbooks for partially seeing children, NAVH became the pioneer and standard setting agency in the preparation of large type.

Today, those publishers who meet our standards carry the prestigious "Seal of Approval" indicating high quality large print. We are delighted that Thorndike Press is one of the publishers whose titles meet these standards. We are also pleased to recognize the significant contribution Thorndike Press is making in this important and growing field.

Lorraine H. Marchi, L.H.D.
Founder/CEO
NAVH

* Thorndike Press encompasses the following imprints: Thorndike, Wheeler, Walker and Large Pr int Press.

Author's Note

The reign of Tsar Alexander III of Russia opened with a persecution of the Jews which was unequalled until fifty years later, when Adolf Hitler assumed power in Germany. He ordered that one third of the Jews in the country must die, one third emigrate and one third assimilate.

This appalling programme resulted in thousands of Jews being murdered and their property confiscated, while 225,000 desolate Jewish families left Russia for Western Europe.

In 1892 the Emperor's brother the Grand Duke Serge, a sadist, evicted thousands of Jewish artisans and small traders from Moscow. Their quarters were surrounded by Cossacks in the middle of the night while police ransacked every home driving the unhappy people out of their beds. Classed as criminals they were forced along the roads to nowhere.

In the summer of 1894 the doctor announced that Alexander III was suffering from Dropsy which was the result of the kidney damage he had suffered in a train disaster. Desperately ill and shrunken to half his size, he lingered however, until 11th November.

His son Nicholas II who the Prince of Wales described as 'weak as water' reigned until 1917. The following year he and his family were assassinated by the Bolsheviks.

chapter one

1894

Warren Wood walked into the *Hôtel* Meurice and made himself known to the Receptionist.

He had not been in Europe for nearly a year and only after the Receptionist had sent for the Manager was he recognised.

"It is delightful to see you again, *Monsieur* Wood!" he said in excellent English, "and I hope you enjoyed your trip abroad."

'Trip' was hardly how Warren Wood would have described his journey through North Africa in which there had been moments of delight but a great deal of acute discomfort, besides times when his life had been in danger.

He was however too glad to be back in Paris to be argumentative, so he merely asked if he could have a room, if possible the one he usually occupied, and if his luggage, which he had left at the *Hôtel* nearly a year ago, could be sent up to him.

All this was promised with a politeness which was characteristic of the French.

Then as he would have turned away from the desk the Manager said:

"I have some correspondence for you, *Monsieur*. Would you like it now, or shall I send it up to your room?"

"I will take it now, if you have it handy."

The Manager disappeared into an inner sanctum and returned with a large packet of letters fastened together with string.

Warren Wood took it, put it under his arm, then waited for the page who was carrying a piece of his small baggage to go ahead and show him the way.

The room, if not the same one in which he had stayed before, was identical and on the Fourth Floor, from which he had a delightful view of the roofs and trees of Paris.

As he stood at the window while the porters brought in his luggage he thought there was nothing so attractive and beautiful as Paris in the sunshine.

High above the houses with their grey shutters, which he thought when driving from the station he would recognise anywhere in the world, rose the Eiffel Tower, nine hundred and eighty-four feet high, which had been completed for the Exhibition which had taken place five years before.

Its metal structure, as one Frenchman Warren had met at the time had boasted, was symbolic of the creativity, vigour and brilliance of France.

But Warren had, at that moment, not been interested in anything else except his own feelings of frustration and despair.

Almost as if the Tower silhouetted against the sky made him remember what he had determined to forget, he turned from the window, tipped the porters who were waiting expectantly, and sat down in an armchair to look at his letters.

He was surprised there were so many and he wondered who, except his mother, could have bothered to write to him after he had left England.

Then as he undid the string and removed the neat band of paper that held the letters together, he looked at the one on top of the pile and stiffened.

For a moment he could hardly credit what he was seeing.

Yet there was no mistaking the flamboyant lettering, the pale blue envelope which was so familiar and the subtle, seductive scent of magnolias which personified the writer.

He stared at the envelope as if it fascinated him, and yet at the same time he was afraid to open it.

Why, he asked himself, should Magnolia, of all people, be writing to him here in Paris?

That she had done so meant that she must have obtained his address from his mother, who was the only person who knew where he would be staying on his journey home.

He told himself that if there was one person he did not wish to hear from at this moment it was Magnolia.

Then with a frown between his eyes and a tightening of his lips he carefully opened the envelope.

Warren Wood was an extremely good-looking young man, but his appearance had altered in the last year from the personification of an elegant 'Man-About-Town' to become more intensely masculine and at the same time harder and more ruthless.

It would have been impossible to live through the experiences he had shared with Edward Duncan without learning that life was not just a round of amusements and pleasure as it had been in the past and could never be the same again.

At times on their journey in Africa

Warren had thought he could not stand it any longer and must admit he was defeated by the elements, the incredibly unpalatable food, and most of all the camels.

If there was one thing Warren had grown to hate it was the camels.

They were lazy, tiresome, unpleasant beasts, difficult to handle, smelt abominably, and at first made him feel sea-sick.

After nearly a year's endurance he had learnt to master them, but he knew that while he loved horses and could not imagine his life without dogs, the camel was undoubtedly his *bête noire*.

He even thought they reminded him of some of his friends and acquaintances and once said to Edward:

"I shall certainly avoid these people in the future!"

Edward had laughed almost derisively. When they left each other the morning before at Marseilles he had said:

"Goodbye Warren! I cannot tell you how much I have enjoyed your company and what a delight it has been to have you with me."

He spoke so sincerely that Warren felt almost embarrassed thinking of the times when he had cursed himself for accepting Edward's invitation.

However, he knew when he looked back on these last months they had enriched his character and broadened his horizons in many ways that he had never anticipated.

And yet now, the first thing he had found on his return was a letter from Magnolia.

And it was Magnolia who was the reason why he had gone to Africa to forget.

He had been sitting in his Club in St. James's with a large glass of brandy beside him when Edward had sat down in an adjacent chair.

"Hello, Warren!" he had said. "I have not seen you for sometime, but then I have been in the country."

"Hello!"

The tone of Warren's voice made Edward look at him sharply.

"What is the matter?" he asked. "I have not seen you look so down in the dumps since you were beaten in the Long Jump at Eton!"

Warren did not reply, he only looked down at the glass beside him and Edward asked in a different tone:

"What has upset you? Can I help?"

"Not unless you can tell me the best way of putting a bullet through my brain!" Warren answered.

His friend looked at him searchingly before he enquired:

"Are you serious?"

"Very! But I suppose if I did shoot myself it would distress my mother, who is the only person I can trust in this damned crooked, filthy world in which everybody lies, and lies, and lies!"

He spoke so violently that Edward glanced around the room hoping he was not being overheard.

Fortunately there were only two other members, elderly and half-asleep, in the big leather chairs at the other end of the room, oblivious to everything except themselves.

"It is not like you to talk like that," Edward remarked. "What has happened?"

Warren had given a bitter laugh and Edward, who had known him since they had been at School and Oxford together, realised he had had a lot to drink, which was for him very unusual, and was at the talkative stage.

"Tell me what is wrong," he said coaxingly.

As if he was glad to have somebody with whom to share his feelings, Warren replied:

"It is not a very original story, but I have just learnt that the only thing that counts is a man's possessions — not himself!"

"You cannot be speaking of Magnolia?" Edward asked tentatively.

"Who else?" Warren replied. "When I took her down to stay at Buckwood it never crossed my mind that she was not, as she had assured me, as much in love with me as I was with her."

He paused and his fingers tightened on his glass as he said fiercely:

"I loved her, Edward, loved her with my whole heart! She was everything I wanted in a woman and as my wife."

"I know that," Edward replied quietly, "but what happened then?"

Again there was that bitter and unpleasant laugh before Warren replied:

"You may well ask! She met Raymond!"

Edward stared at him.

"Do you mean your cousin? But, good Heavens, he has only just come of age!"

"What did that matter, beside the fact that he is an Earl?"

In a mocking, sarcastic voice Warren went on:

"My dear Edward, you must realise, as I was stupid enough not to do, that all a woman needs to make her happy is a title and money. What the man himself is like is utterly and completely immaterial!"

16

Edward would have spoken, but Warren continued:

"He may have bow legs, crossed eyes, warts on his nose, but if he is likely to become a Marquis, then the idea of being his wife supercedes every other feeling in what she quite erroneously describes as her — heart!"

He choked over the last word and drained what was left in his glass, then put up his hand to attract a waiter.

Fortunately there was not one in the room at the moment and Edward said:

"Before you get too drunk, Warren, tell me the whole story. I am not only interested, but very sympathetic."

"Thank you, old boy!" Warren replied. "I suppose I can trust you not to let me down, although I swear to God I will never trust a woman again — never!"

"But surely," Edward protested, "Magnolia does not intend to marry Raymond?"

"Oh, yes, she does!" Warren replied. "And now I look back, I realise she made a dead set for him the very moment we walked into Buckwood! I suppose, now I think about it, Raymond had not got a chance as soon as she looked at him with her large dewy eyes!"

Edward knew this was very likely true.

Magnolia Keane was not only beautiful, but she had practised the art of fascinating men until, as Edward was well aware, she could exert an almost hypnotic influence on anyone she desired.

He had known quite a lot about Magnolia before she met his friend Warren Wood, and the first time he saw them together he had thought it a mistake for him to become embroiled with her.

Coming from a good county family, Magnolia had come to London determined to find herself a rich and important husband.

It should have been easy, Edward thought, considering how extremely beautiful she was, while her father, who was Master of a well-known pack of foxhounds, was popular and had a number of friends in sporting circles.

But Magnolia's father was not a rich man, and while by a great deal of scrimping and saving Colonel Keane could afford to take a house in London for the Season, it was not in the most fashionable area, and he did not contemplate giving a Ball for his daughter.

This meant that invitations she received were not as numerous as they would have been if she had been able to reciprocate in the usual manner.

The whole process of bringing out a débutante was very much a 'cutlet for a cutlet' and Colonel and Mrs. Keane and their daughter Magnolia had not been invited to any Balls given by the leaders of London Society!

This therefore resulted in Magnolia meeting many fewer eligible bachelors than she had hoped.

She did not, in fact, receive a single proposal of marriage during her first Season, and although a great many men admired her, unfortunately most of them were already married.

In consequence the Dowagers gossiped about her and her name was crossed off a number of lists which every hostess kept punctiliously.

The following year, after having shone like a star at a number of Hunt Balls and attended Race-Meetings and Point-to-Points at which she was inevitably encircled by a group of admiring men, both old and young, Magnolia came to London again.

She was determined that this time she would end the Season with an engagement ring on her finger.

There was no engagement ring, but she

did meet a distinguished Baronet eighteen years her senior, who became her constant companion and in private pursued her as relentlessly as any hound pursued a fox.

Magnolia played him skilfully as a fisherman would play what appeared to be a hooked fish, but at the last moment, when she had actually started to plan her trousseau, he got away.

She could hardly believe it was true when he told her that he had made some extremely bad investments and found it would be impossible for him to keep up his house and estates unless, to put it bluntly, he 'married money.'

Magnolia decided to put a good face on what was a disastrous set-back and a humiliation she was determined not to acknowledge.

The moment she realised she had lost her Baronet, she told her friends most convincingly that she had found it impossible to marry a man who was so much older than herself and 'set in his ways.'

"It may be very stupid of me," she had said, "but I want somebody I can not only love, but also laugh with, and enjoy life as poor James found it impossible to do."

If a few people guessed the truth, the majority merely assumed that as Magnolia was so beautiful she had plenty of time to find somebody who really suited her.

Only Magnolia herself was aware that time was passing, and if she was not careful she would find herself 'on the shelf.'

She was well aware that most men married a girl because she was young and innocent, and what they thought of as an ideal wife.

If they wanted anything else, there were always the sophisticated Beauties who were to be found in the 'Marlborough House Set,' and who were acclaimed wherever they went by the public and in the newspapers.

At nearly twenty-one Magnolia was desperate when she met Warren Wood.

He was everything that she thought a man should be, handsome, exceedingly well-bred and welcome in the most distinguished Social Circles.

His father, Lord John Wood, was the younger brother of the Marquis of Buckwood and, as Magnolia was well aware, there was no family in the whole of the British Isles more respected and admired than that headed by the Marquis.

The house from which the first Marquis had taken his name stood on an estate which had been given by Queen Elizabeth to Sir Walter Wood after he had sunk three Spanish galleons.

He had brought her not only the spoils of victory, but also some exceedingly fine pearls which he had taken from his prisoners.

As soon as Magnolia met Warren she told herself he was her fate.

Although as far as she could ascertain he did not have much money, she knew that every Social door would be open to her as his wife and she would undoubtedly embellish the 'Marlborough House Set.'

Warren who at twenty-eight had enjoyed a great number of love-affairs with the Beauties who found him both handsome and charming, was surprisingly bowled over by Magnolia.

There was something irresistible, he thought, about her large, dark liquid eyes, and her soft white skin which really did have the texture of a magnolia.

It was only later that he learnt that she had not in fact been christened 'Magnolia,' but the more commonplace 'Mary,' but had changed to a more glamorous name when she was old enough to appreciate her own charms.

She was in fact very beautiful and attractive, and had, when she wanted to use it, a charm that few people especially men could resist.

Unfortunately for Magnolia at the time when he proposed her mother had died most inconveniently two months earlier.

This meant that it would be considered extremely improper and heartless for her even to think of an engagement until at least four more months had elapsed.

Then they would still have to wait another three months before they could be married.

Magnolia had no intention of starting her marriage off on the wrong foot from a social point of view.

She had therefore accepted Warren's proposal with alacrity, but told him that for the time being it must be a precious secret between the two of them.

"I understand, my darling," he said, "and of course I will do anything you want, except that I cannot wait one moment longer than is absolutely necessary to make you my wife."

"I love you! I love you!" Magnolia had said. "If it is difficult for you to wait, it is equally as hard for me!"

He thought nobody could be more adorable as he kissed her passionately and she had appeared a little shy.

Then she had extricated herself from his arms while still holding closely to his hand.

"We must be very careful that we are not talked about," she said. "At the same time, darling, wonderful Warren, I would love to meet your family."

He smiled.

"I expect really you want to see Buckwood!" he said. "It is the most beautiful house in the world, and I only wish for your sake that I owned it!"

He laughed before he continued:

"It would become you, and I could not pay you a higher compliment!"

He had then explained to her that his uncle was extremely kind to him, and although his parents lived in a charming old Manor House on the estate, he was allowed to use Buckwood as if it was his own home, to ride his uncle's horses and to shoot in his woods.

"We are a very close family," he said, "and I know that Uncle Arthur will love you, as he loved my father."

Lord John had died about fifteen months ago, and Warren missed his father so desperately that he had instinctively put his uncle in his father's place.

He was quite certain his uncle would

find Magnolia as lovely and as charming as he did himself. At the same time, he wanted his approval and he therefore took her down to Buckwood at the first opportunity.

They stayed of course in the Manor House with his mother.

While he thought she was a little cooler than he would have liked towards Magnolia, he put it down to the fact that, although she wanted him to marry, she was understandably over-anxious as to whether any woman would make him as happy as she wanted him to be.

The Marquis however had found Magnolia just as charming as Warren had anticipated.

Because Magnolia told him to keep secret the fact that they were engaged, Warren had merely hinted to his uncle that he might be considering 'popping the question' and asked his advice.

"A very pretty girl, my dear boy!" the Marquis had said. "Very pretty! I hope she likes the idea of living in the country. She is no use to you otherwise."

"She was brought up in the country," Warren had replied, "and her father is Master of the Ferriers."

"So you told me, so you told me," the

Marquis said, "and I think I have met him. Nice chap. Well, his daughter should certainly be able to ride to hounds."

"She can certainly do that!" Warren enthused.

At the same time, although he hated to admit it, when he saw Magnolia on a horse he was not as impressed as he had thought he would be.

He had the idea she was nervous and, although it had never crossed his mind before, that she was afraid of falling and damaging her lovely face.

This however was a very minor flaw in somebody who otherwise appeared to be absolutely perfect.

There were a number of guests as usual staying at Buckwood who were the Marquis's friends, and almost as soon as they arrived Raymond appeared with three of his.

They had just come down from Oxford and were in tremendously high spirits, noisy and ready for any sort of 'fun,' from tobogganing downstairs on tea trays to playing practical jokes on each other and of course on Magnolia.

She responded to them in a way that made Warren admire her more than he had done before.

It seemed to him excellent that instead of moving with a certain dignity and grace as she had in London, and competing on their own ground with women much older than herself, she could enter wholeheartedly into the laughter and fun of the young men who teased her as if she was a pretty kitten.

It was freezing weather and the next day when the ice on the lake was bearing, skates were produced for everybody as if by magic and it did not surprise Warren that Magnolia was an excellent skater.

She certainly looked exquisite on the ice, her slim figure showing to its best advantage when she was on skates, and her dark hair and large eyes framed by a fur hat of white fox.

The young men fought with each other as to who should skate with her next, and usually there was one on each side of her as they sped over the ice at what seemed remarkable speed.

Warren had watched them benignly.

He enjoyed skating but had no wish to indulge in acrobatics, and later in the day left them to enjoy themselves while he went riding with his uncle.

The Marquis had grown very stout in his old age and liked to take things easy.

27

As they rode over the Park they talked of the estate and the steps he had taken to have everything working in perfect order for when Raymond should inherit it.

"I wish he would take a little more interest in what I am doing," the Marquis said. "When you have a chance, Warren, have a talk with him and make him see that an estate of this size depends entirely on its owner taking a personal interest in everything that is done and in every person who is employed to do it."

"I am sure Raymond appreciates that, Uncle Arthur," Warren replied. "But he is still very young, and I thought this morning he and his friends were more like a lot of puppies playing with each other. I am sure in time he will settle down and learn to be as good a landowner as you are."

"I hope so, I sincerely hope so," the Marquis muttered.

Then as if he wished to change the subject he went on:

"I want to talk to you about this new tenant of ours. I am not sure if I have put the right man in charge of . . ."

It was quite late as they returned to Buckwood.

It was almost dark, and the skaters had

gone in and were now playing some mad game around the billiard-table which resulted in a lot of joking, and what Warren privately thought of as 'horse-play.'

Magnolia seemed happy, and he thought how lovely she looked with her cheeks flushed, her hair a little dishevelled.

He wanted to take her in his arms and kiss her, but when he tried to draw her away from the others she told him in a whisper that she thought it would be a mistake for them to disappear together.

"I love you, darling," she said softly, "but we must be very, very careful!"

He understood, and instead went to the Study to read the newspapers which had arrived from London.

He thought as he did so how lucky he was to have found somebody so adaptable that she would undoubtedly make him a perfect wife.

It was four days later, when he was taking Magnolia back to London that the bomb-shell fell.

When he thought back he realised he must have been both stupid and blind not to realise what was happening.

There had been dancing in the evenings with young people coming in from neighbouring houses at Raymond's invitation, some staying, the others arriving after dinner.

He had organised it all very skilfully.

Besides the more formal dancing when Magnolia waltzed with Warren, there were also a noisy Lancers, Quadrilles and Scottish Reels which usually resulted in girls being swung off their feet amid screams of delight.

It all seemed very young and amusing, but it had passed through Warren's mind that he was getting rather old for so much ragging.

Nevertheless the Prince of Wales had started the fashion for practical jokes and a great deal of 'horse-play' in the parties he had enjoyed a few years earlier.

Now he had begun to prefer the Bridge table.

It was only when he saw Raymond whispering to Magnolia the night before they returned to London that he wondered what they had to say to each other, but was glad they could be such good friends.

Then as they travelled back alone in a reserved carriage with Magnolia's maid in the next-door compartment she said a little tentatively:

"I have something to tell you, Warren."

"What is it, my precious?" he asked.

"And have I told you how beautiful you look today? Every time I see you, you are lovelier than yesterday!"

"Thank you," she replied, "but I want you to understand that while I still love you, I cannot marry you!"

"What do you mean?" Warren asked.

He spoke sharply because he was so astonished, and then thought he could not have heard her aright.

She raised her eyes pleadingly to him as she said:

"I do not want you to be angry with me."

"Of course I will not be angry with you!" he replied. "How could I be? But I do not understand what you are saying!"

"I am saying, dear Warren, that while I love you, I am going to marry Raymond!"

Warren just stared at her, feeling as though his head was suddenly filled with cotton-wool and he could not take in what she was saying.

At length, in a voice that did not sound like his own he ejaculated:

"Marry Raymond? How can you? He only came of age last November!"

"He wants to marry me, but of course we shall have to wait until I am out of mourning."

"And you really think you can do this to me?" Warren managed to ask, the words coming jerkily from between his lips.

"I am sorry, dear Warren, but you have to understand."

"What have I to understand?"

She hesitated. Then he knew the answer.

"You mean that Raymond will one day become the Marquis of Buckwood!"

"You did say yourself that the house would become me!"

"So that is how it is!"

He felt as if the train was spinning dizzily round him.

Then as he realised they were drawing into Paddington Station he knew that Magnolia had timed her revelation very cleverly to coincide with their arrival.

A minute later the carriage-door was opened by a Porter, Magnolia's lady's-maid appeared, and there was no more time for intimate discussion.

Her closed carriage was waiting outside, and as they reached it Warren raised his hat to Magnolia, then walked away.

He had not spoken one single word since they left the train.

Only as he climbed into a hired hansom and directed it to drive to his Club was he aware that he was shaking with anger.

At the same time a desperate sense of loss pervaded him making him feel as if the very sky had caved in on his head.

He had loved Magnolia, he had loved her in a way he had never loved anybody before, and he had believed in her protestations of love.

Now scraps of conversation were coming back to him.

"I am afraid we shall not be at all rich, my precious," he had said. "Although my father had an unusually generous allowance from my uncle, I still have to provide for my mother."

"I love you because you are you!" Magnolia had said in her soft, sweet voice. "If you had not a penny in the world I would love you just the same!"

"Darling, could anybody be more wonderful?"

On another occasion he said:

"As soon as you allow me to tell my uncle we are engaged, I know he will offer us a house somewhere on the estate. There are quite a number of small, attractive Manors which I know you will make look very lovely."

"What I want to do is to make a home for you."

"I know you will do that," Warren an-

33

swered, "and of course we will try to afford to have a small house in London as well."

"I hope it will be big enough for me to entertain your friends," she said. "Just because we are married, I must not deprive you of all the people who love you because you are so wonderful. But I know the women will be very envious of me for having such a clever, handsome and attractive husband."

"We will buy a house with a large Dining-Room and a large Drawing-Room," Warren promised.

At the same time, he wondered if he would be able to afford it.

Because he loved Magnolia he had already begun to economise, so that he could save money to buy her all the things she would want once she was his wife.

Fortunately, because he did have so many rich and what she called 'important' friends, he knew they would stay away a lot in house-parties, where he had always been welcomed in the past.

That would mean she would require a number of glamorous gowns, and he told himself he would have to curtail some of the small extravagances with which he had indulged himself as a bachelor.

However, because he loved Magnolia he

felt that nothing could be too great a sacrifice, and he felt as if he wanted to lay himself and everything that belonged to him as a tribute at her feet.

Now he could hardly believe that, loving him as she had said she did, she could marry a boy who was hardly any older than herself and, as Warren knew, very young and in his own way, unfledged.

Raymond was not at all intelligent and had very few positive attributes except for a straight-forward character and a youthful desire to enjoy himself without worrying about anything else.

The Marquis was, although he had never admitted it, slightly disappointed in his son. Raymond's reports at School had not been good, and he had twice nearly been sent down from Oxford for making no effort to study.

Then when his father tried to teach him about the estate, Raymond showed no real interest in it, except for the amusement it could afford him.

Warren had never really thought of Raymond as being grown up and certainly not as anybody's husband, let alone Magnolia's.

To think that she was marrying him just because he would one day be the Marquis of Buckwood made him feel appalled, disgusted, and at the same time humiliated that he still loved her, still desired her, and felt that life was insupportable without her.

By the time he had reached his Club and drunk an inordinate amount of brandy he told himself that it was not a question of wondering how he could live without her, but more that he did not intend to do so.

It was then that Edward had found him.

"Now listen, Warren," he said, "I have a suggestion to make, and I want you to consider it seriously."

"The most sensible thing I can do is to jump into the Thames!" Warren replied somewhat thickly. "I am not likely to drown because I am a strong swimmer, but I may die of the cold!"

"I have a better suggestion."

"What is it?"

The question was surly and Edward replied:

"You can come with me to Africa!"

"To Africa?"

There was just a note of surprise in the question which made Edward think he was at least curious.

"I am going there to find material for a new book," he said. "I am also going to explore parts of the desert and Morocco

36

where few people, and I imagine no Englishman, has ever been before. We might have some game-hunting too. We could also lose ourselves in a sandstorm or be killed by some hostile tribe!"

"That would solve my problem, at any rate!" Warren remarked.

"I agree it would save a lot of trouble and be an interesting and unusual way to die."

There was silence. Then Edward said:

"Come with me! I do not think you will regret it, and at least you will not have to sit here crying over Magnolia and wondering what she is doing with Raymond."

He paused before he added:

"You are much more likely to be fending off reptiles or other dangerous animals and thinking of how draughty and uncomfortable it is in a tent which is likely to blow away at any moment!"

"You certainly make it sound very unattractive!"

"I cannot promise you a feather-bed or the exotic pleasures of the East!" Edward replied. "But it will give you something to fight, and I think that is what you really need at this particular moment."

There was silence.

Then as if Warren was seeing Magnolia and hating her with a violence which could only come from a man who had been 'crossed in love,' he said:

"All right, if you want me, I will come with you. But you must make all the arrangements, while I become disgustingly and I hope obliviously, drunk!"

Thinking back, Warren could hear himself saying it, and while he spoke, despising himself for being so weak, so stupid as to love a woman who had rejected him for a title.

And yet now, a year later, the letter he was holding in his hand seemed to disturb something within him that he thought he had forgotten.

As he looked down at the letter he could smell Magnolia's perfume coming from it, and he could remember as he looked at the curves of the letters she had written, the curves of her breasts and the smallness of her waist.

He thought he could feel the warmth of her lips beneath his which had made not only his heart beat faster but also hers.

He had known that if he desired her as a woman, she also desired him as a man.

"Magnolia! Magnolia!"

His whole body cried out for her.

But why the hell had she written to him now?

chapter two

For a moment the words on the blue writing-paper seemed to dance in front of Warren's eyes.

Then he read:

"Dearest, Most Beloved Warren,

How could you have gone away so cruelly without telling me where you were going? I could not believe it when I learnt you had left England.

I knew then how foolish I was and that I had been swept away by a sort of madness which I cannot explain, but which I think made me temporarily insane!

Now I have had time to think it over I know there is only one man in my life and that is you!

I love you, and I can only beg you on my knees if necessary, to forgive me.

I cannot believe that I have really lost something so precious, so marvellous, as your love. My only excuse for not appreciating it was that I had never known anybody like you before.

Your uncle tells me you are somewhere in Africa and he has no address, so I can therefore only send this letter to Paris where I have learnt you will stay first when you return.

When you read it, darling, forget my stupidity and think only of how happy we were before we went to Buckwood, and let me once again creep into your heart.

Forgive me and let us know the bliss we both felt when you first kissed me.

I love you! I love you!

Your very penitent and humble
Magnolia."

Having read the letter Warren stared at it as if he could not believe his eyes.

He looked at the date and saw that it had been written nine months ago, in fact only a month after he had left England.

It really did not seem possible that Magnolia should have changed her mind so completely and so quickly, and because it seemed incredible he read her letter over again.

He felt he must find some explanation, although what it could be he had no idea.

He looked through the pile of letters and under several bills and half-a-dozen what he guessed were invitations, all of which had been sent to White's Club in London and forwarded on, he found a letter addressed directly to the *Hôtel* from his mother.

He thought as he looked at her neat, aristocratic writing that it was very different from Magnolia's somewhat flamboyant style.

But having no wish to criticise, he opened his mother's letter and read:

"My darling son,

I was so delighted to receive a letter from you yesterday from Casablanca to tell me you were on your way home.

I have been desperately anxious to get in touch with you, and it seemed almost an answer to my prayers that you should have written to tell me that it would not be long before you are in England again.

What is important is that as soon as you receive this letter you should come home immediately.

I know that you will be extremely

upset and sad to learn that Raymond had a fall out riding three days ago and I have just learnt that he died this morning from his injuries.

It was apparently in some wild midnight Steeple-Chase in which he was taking part when staying with a friend and I think all the competitors had enjoyed a very good dinner and perhaps too much to drink.

Now poor Raymond is dead, and Dr. Gregory, who came to tell me what he had just learnt, also brought the grave news that your Uncle Arthur has had a heart-attack.

He has not been well for the last few months owing to the fact that he is so over-weight. On top of this, the news of Raymond's accident had been too much for him.

He is in a coma, although still alive, but Dr. Gregory says frankly there is little chance of his recovering.

You will therefore understand, Dearest Warren, that you are needed here urgently, and I can only pray that you will get this letter quickly. Please telegraph me when you receive it.

I am so sorry that your home-coming should be spoilt by such unhappy news, and the sense of loss which we will both feel.

At the same time, I know that you will take over your responsibilities and perform them conscientiously with the same dignity and compassion that was so characteristic of your father.

Bless you, my darling son, I am waiting anxiously to hear from you.

Your devoted
and affectionate mother,
Elizabeth Wood."

If Warren had been shocked and surprised by Magnolia's letter, his mother's left him gasping.

He could not believe it possible that his Cousin Raymond, so young and full of life, should be dead, or that his Uncle should not be expected to live.

He realised that in consequence his whole life had changed while at the same time he could hardly credit that what his mother told him was true.

He had never in his wildest dreams ever thought of himself as being the Marquis of Buckwood.

Just as he knew it had never crossed his father's mind that he might have inherited instead of his brother.

Lord John had no ambitions of that sort, nor had he an ounce of envy in his whole body.

"No one could be a better head of the family than Arthur," he would say frequently.

When he was ill and aware that he might not recover from what had been a very serious operation, he had said to Warren:

"Look after your mother, and help Arthur in every way you can. I know that he relies on you."

"Yes, of course, Papa," Warren replied.

His father had given him a faint smile.

"You are a good son, Warren," he said faintly. "I have always been very proud of you!"

As he remembered his father's words Warren could not help wishing that he could have taken his brother's place.

Then he found himself wondering who would help him to carry on as head of the family.

He was well aware how many Woods there were who would look to him for help and guidance and to do honour to the family name.

Just for a moment the hugeness of the task which had suddenly been thrust upon him seemed almost overwhelming.

There were not only huge estates in many parts of England for which he would be responsible, but also Orphanages, Alms Houses, Schools and so many Charities that the list of them, as he knew, filled three pages of foolscap.

There were also the hereditary duties of the Marquis of Buckwood at Court, and he was well aware that Queen Victoria had a soft place in her heart for his uncle and frequently had demanded his presence at Windsor Castle so that she could ask his advice.

When Warren thought of the Queen it was almost as if he drew himself to attention.

He not only respected but also fervently admired Her Majesty and he recognised how much the expansion and prosperity and prestige of the British Empire owed to her presence and the manner in which she inspired those who served her.

Then he remembered how urgent his mother's need of him was and he looked at her letter again and found that she had written it three days ago.

"I must leave for England first thing in the morning," he told himself, and thought he would ask the Concierge for the times of the boat-trains from the *Gare du Nord*.

He would at the same time ask for a Telegraph Form with which he could relieve his mother's anxiety by saying he was on his way.

Then as he pushed aside the rest of his correspondence he saw that the *Hôtel* had written a date on his mother's envelope which told him it had arrived yesterday, two days after she had written it.

Written quite clearly was: *"June 27th"* with the seven crossed in the foreign fashion.

It was then an idea came to him and he picked up Magnolia's envelope which lay on the floor at his feet.

Written on that, also by the *Hôtel* was: *"June 27th"*.

For a moment he stared at it as if he could hardly believe his eyes.

Then he referred to Magnolia's letter on which there was engraved the date quite clearly: *"October 20th 1893"*.

Then he understood, and for a moment the cynical lines around his mouth made him look older and almost unpleasant.

He told himself it was what he might have expected, that Magnolia, the moment Raymond was dead, had tried to make sure of him.

Because the idea of such perfidy made him feel murderous he threw her letter down on the floor, and walking to the window stood looking out with unseeing eyes.

The sun was sinking and the last dying glow over the roofs of Paris was breathtakingly beautiful.

But Warren was only seeing Magnolia's lovely face as she concocted her plot to make herself the Marchioness of Buckwood, by hook or by crook.

He wanted to kill her.

How could any woman he had once loved behave in such an appalling manner or imagine that he would be deceived by such lies?

He knew as he stood there that the last vestige of feeling he had for Magnolia had finally been driven out of him as if by the thrust of a knife.

Now he knew that even if she was kneeling at his feet and looking up at him imploringly with her large, dark, liquid eyes, his only impulse would be to strike her.

He felt he could almost see her crafty brain at work when she realised that having lost Raymond she must now win him back at all costs.

She had, therefore, concocted what had seemed a very clever plan of sending him a letter which purported to have been written almost as soon as he had gone abroad.

If the *Hôtel* had not been so punctilious about marking the post as it arrived, he might never have guessed that what she had written was not a genuine change of heart when she had learnt that he had gone abroad.

In order to make sure that he was not making a mistake, he looked at the other letters he had received and saw on each one of them the date of their arrival scrawled by the Concierge.

He had not himself, actually given instructions regarding his mail to the secretary of White's Club, but he knew that Edward had ordered his letters to be sent to Paris and he supposed he had made the same arrangement for him.

The only person to whom he himself had given this address was his mother, and he wondered how Magnolia had extracted the information from her without her being suspicious of what she was about to do.

Then he had another idea, and looking amongst the pile of letters now scattered on the floor he found one he suspected might be there.

It was dated, as his mother's had been, three days earlier and was from his uncle's Solicitors in the neighbouring County Town. He guessed it was from them that Magnolia had obtained his address in Paris, and that they had got it from his mother.

The Solicitors' letter was signed by a Partner he knew well, who had been a friend also of his father's.

He conveyed his deepest sympathy and his regret at having to inform him of his Cousin Raymond's death.

He asked him to return as soon as he received the letter as it was important he should attend to all the things appertaining to the estate which at the moment his uncle was unable to do.

It was quite obvious from what Warren read that the Solicitor, like his mother, thought there was no hope for the Marquis, and he felt as if they were placing the burden of authority on his shoulders almost before his uncle was buried.

Then as he laid the Solicitors' letter tidily down on a table, he deliberately put his foot down hard on Magnolia's sheet of blue writing-paper, pressing it brutally into the carpet.

The moon was high in the sky and the

stars were shining like diamonds as Warren walked along the bank of the River Seine.

When he was in Africa with Edward they had sometimes talked of what they would do when they got back to civilisation.

"We will stay a few days in Paris, old boy," Edward had said. "I have always found it is the right place to 'bridge the gap' between the primitive and the sophisticated."

Warren had looked at the desert stretching away to a lazy horizon so that it was difficult to know where the sand ended and the sky began.

"I suppose," he said mockingly, "you are thinking of the *Moulin Rouge* and *Maxim's!*"

"When I am on a journey like this," Edward replied, "I find myself almost forgetting what an attractive woman looks like! I would certainly welcome one of the Sirens from *Maxim's* at the moment and enjoy seeing the girls kicking their legs in the 'Can-Can' at the *Moulin Rouge*."

Warren had laughed. Then he said:

"What I would like is a glass of cold champagne! If I have to drink water out of a goat's-skin very much longer, I think I shall go mad!"

"You would certainly go mad without it!" Edward retorted glancing up at the blazing sun overhead.

They had been trekking for nearly four days and, as Warren had said, the water they drank from the goat's-skin grew daily more and more unpleasant.

"Tomorrow we will be able to replenish our stores," Edward said. "Although I am afraid it will not be like the food we could enjoy at one of those expensive Restaurants in the *Palais Royal*. And after all the privations you are suffering at the moment, your clothes will need inches taken in before you can wear them again."

Warren had laughed, but he knew when he changed for dinner tonight that Edward had been right.

His clothes, if they were to fit as perfectly as they had before he had left for Africa, would certainly need the attention of an experienced Tailor.

At the same time, his muscles were harder and he had a feeling, although of course it was absurd, that his shoulders were broader.

But he knew the endless hours of riding either one of the desert horses or a camel had resulted in his body becoming athletically stronger, despite the fact that the food he had eaten had been rather to keep him alive than for enjoyment.

In spite of all he had to ponder over he could not help appreciating the excellent dinner he had eaten at a small Restaurant not far from the *Hôtel*.

He remembered thinking vaguely that if he had not been so worried about what was waiting for him at home, he might have looked up a very attractive lady with whom he had spent several delightful evenings when he had stayed in Paris previously.

When he had passed through it with Edward on his way to Africa, he had merely deposited his clothes at the *Hôtel* and because he was feeling so knocked out by Magnolia he had let Edward choose what they should do that evening.

They had started at the *Folies Bergères* but he had left Edward at *Maxim's* without even dancing with one of the extremely alluring hostesses.

Although in Africa he had had very different ideas about what he would do on this first night in Paris, now he only wanted to think, and he had therefore eaten alone and as it was warm he decided to walk before he retired to bed.

The *Hôtel* had found him an Express train which connected with a steamer leaving Calais at midday, and he calculated that if he was fortunate he could arrive at his mother's late that evening.

He therefore telegraphed her to say that he would be with her at about ten o'clock, but not to worry if it was later.

It was all a question of timing, but in the summer there was less chance of being delayed on the Cross-Channel Steamer than there was at other times of the year when the sea might be rough.

Tonight there was not even a breath of wind or the rustle of leaves in the trees that bordered the river.

Warren walking slowly beneath them thought the moonlight shining on the great buildings and turning their roofs to silver was very different from the moonlight that had percolated through the palm trees of an oasis where they had slept when they could find one.

At other times, when they erected their tent amongst stones and rough shrubs they had had to be wary of snakes, scorpions and the innumerable unpleasant insects which all seemed to have an irresistible desire to creep into his sleeping-bag or down the back of his neck.

He thought now with a twisted smile that the clip-clop of the horses' hoofs moving down the tarmacked roads were very different from the grunts of the camels, and the coarse manner in which their Arab servants would clear their throats before they spat.

'This is civilisation,' he thought.

He felt as if it was like silk in which he could wrap himself after wearing sackcloth for a long time.

He crossed over a bridge so that he could look at *Nôtre Dame* with the moon shining on the Seine beneath it.

He was remembering how when he had first come to Paris as a very young man, he had stayed on the Left Bank because everything there was so much cheaper.

He recalled how, on leaving his *Hôtel* and walking towards the Seine, the first thing he had seen was *Nôtre Dame* and he had found the ancient Cathedral irresistibly romantic.

He leaned his arms on the cool stones of a wall which bordered the great river and watched a barge with its red and green lights reflected in the water, passing slowly downstream.

It was then he became aware that there was somebody below him on the tow-path which had been built for the horses which pulled every barge that passed through Paris towards their destinations.

Without really paying attention he noticed the slim figure of what appeared to be a very young girl moving along the edge of the water and looking down into it.

Strangely she was not wearing a hat or even a shawl over her head, and the moonlight seemed to touch her hair with silver.

Warren watched her while he was still thinking about himself, noticing that she had a grace that made her move almost as if she was walking on the water rather than on the ground, and that her waist was very small.

Then as she reached the shadows of the bridge she stood looking with a curious intentness.

Almost unconsciously, but with the perception of a man who has lived with danger and becomes aware of it almost before it happens, Warren knew what she was about to do.

It was not that she moved or even bent forward; she just stood looking into the water, and he was aware almost as if someone told him that she was choosing her moment.

Without really thinking, without considering that he did not wish to be involved, Warren walked quickly to the opening in the wall just beside the bridge from which steps led down to the tow-path.

They ended only a few feet from where the girl was standing.

Moving silently because he was wearing soft-soled evening pumps, Warren reached her side.

Deep in her thoughts she was unaware of him and he said quietly, so as not to startle her:

"*Faites attention, Mademoiselle! Ici la Seine est dangereuse.*"

He watched her as he spoke, and the girl stiffened.

Then in a voice as if the words were jerked from between her lips, she said:

"Go . . . away! Leave me . . . alone!"

To Warren's surprise she spoke in English and he answered in the same language:

"How can you think of doing anything so foolish?"

"Why should you . . . care?"

"Some *Gendarme* is bound to see you, and then you will be in trouble."

He still spoke very quietly, and now the girl turned to look at him.

In the shadows he was aware of a small, white pointed face with two huge eyes that seemed to fill it.

She looked at him and he thought, although he was not sure, that she was surprised that he was in evening-dress.

Then she said, still speaking in English:

"Go away! It is no . . . business of . . . yours!"

"As we are of the same nationality, I find that hard to believe."

"Please . . . please . . . leave me alone!"

Now her voice held a hopeless, pleading note in it and he said:

"You say it is none of my business, but because I am English I should feel obliged, if I saw a dog or a cat struggling in the river, to try to save it, and I have no wish to get wet!"

"Then let me die in my . . . own way . . . without . . . interference!"

Her words were very low and, Warren thought, there was a lost note in them that had not been there before.

"So you want to die," he said reflectively. "That is what I wanted to do nine months ago, but a friend prevented me from doing so, and now I am glad to be alive."

"It is different for you . . . you are a man!"

"I am still a human being, and where I have just come from human beings have to fight to live. It has made me appreciate life in a way I never did before."

"Go away!"

She turned her face away from him and he could see her profile silhouetted against the water and thought, although he was not certain, that she was attractive.

At the same time there was something about the sharpness of her chin that made him think she was unnaturally slender.

"Because I was saved by a friend from doing what you are contemplating doing," he said, "I suggest we sit down somewhere, preferably with a glass of wine, and you tell me why you are taking such a desperate step."

As he spoke he saw her whole body stiffen and she said quickly:

"I have told you to go away . . . if you want a woman . . . there are . . . plenty of them in the . . . streets."

It was the obvious interpretation she could put on what he had just said, and Warren said quickly:

"I swear to you, I was not thinking about you like that! If I wanted what you suggest Paris caters for it without my having to come to a tow-path on the Seine!"

He spoke as he might have done to a rather foolish child, and as if she understood she said:

"I apologise . . . that was rude . . . when you are trying to be . . . kind."

"You must be aware it is the sort of thing you must expect if you walk about Paris late at night alone."

"I am not walking about Paris," she said fiercely. "I came here to . . . drown myself . . . and you are preventing me from doing what I . . . want to do."

"As I have already pointed out, it is unlikely you will be successful. Suppose you consider my suggestion and talk it over with someone who has once been in exactly the same position as you are?"

"I doubt that very much."

"It is true, and I really feel it is fate that I should have seen you and known what you were about to do."

"How . . . did you know?"

The question was curious and Warren answered it truthfully:

"I was aware you were in danger just as a month or two ago I was aware that I and the man with whom I was travelling were in danger before it actually occurred. My instinct, or whatever you like to call it, saved our lives in the same way that I have been able to save yours."

The girl to whom he was speaking gave a little sigh.

Then she turned from the river and took a step away from it as if she realised that

59

what she had intended was for the moment at any rate impossible.

They walked side by side up the steps to the road, and now in the moonlight Warren looked at her and realised she was very young — in fact so young that despite the fact that her hair was heaped on top of her head, he thought she was only a child.

Then he realised that she was too tall to be so immature and that the illusion of childishness was caused by the fact that she was so pitifully thin.

She was a replica of some pitiful sights he had seen amongst some of the tribes of Africa, and was obviously suffering from malnutrition.

It was an explanation anyway for her wishing to die, but he merely said:

"There is a small Restaurant near here where I used to eat when I was young. If it is still open I suggest we go there while you tell me about yourself."

"I have no intention of telling you anything, so perhaps I should not accept your . . . invitation under . . . false pretences."

"Then I will talk," Warren said, "and you can listen!"

The girl stood for a moment undecided, as if she thought it might be wiser to run away from him.

Once again he knew what she was thinking and he said:

"As it happens, I would like to talk to you, because I have a tremendous problem on my mind. It is one that would not have been helped by the music and the laughter that I could have found across the river, and that is why I was walking here. You may in fact, be the 'guiding light' for which I was seeking."

"You do not look as if you had any problems," the girl remarked.

He knew as they walked under the light from the street-lamps that she was impressed by the smartness of his white shirt front and long-tailed evening-coat.

"You would be surprised at those with which I have suddenly been confronted!" he said. "So please do as I ask, and I promise that when you want me to escort you back to wherever you are staying I will do so — immediately."

He felt a little shudder go through her as if his words evoked something unpleasant.

Then he crossed the road and walked a little way further before there was a turning where he remembered the Restaurant had been.

He found it was open, but the tables outside on the pavement under a red and white striped awning were empty.

Inside there were half-a-dozen customers seated at tables in the centre of the room, while those at the side where there were sofas against the wall were empty.

At the sight of Warren in evening-dress the Proprietor hurried forward and led him to a sofa-table in a corner.

As they sat down Warren was aware as the girl seated herself beside him that surprisingly she was not embarrassed by her surroundings, nor by the fact that she was without a wrap or gloves.

Then he noticed that the gown she was wearing was threadbare. She had a long, swan-like neck, and he thought if she was not so thin she would be very attractive.

She made no attempt to look at the menu which the Proprietor put in front of her at the same time as he handed one to Warren.

"Shall I order?" he asked.

"Thank you."

Glancing at her without appearing to be too curious he realised he had been right in thinking she was suffering from lack of food and was in fact, near to starvation.

He could see the prominent bones at her wrists, the thinness of her fingers and, as he had noticed before, the sharp line of her chin.

Her eyes were unnaturally large and he knew she was remarkably pretty, in fact the right word was 'lovely.'

Knowing it would be ready he ordered first some vichyssoise, a cold soup which was nourishing because it was made of potatoes and cream.

Then he ordered a chicken dish which the Proprietor informed him was the *Spécialité de la Maison.*

"I think I remember it when I came here many years ago," Warren remarked.

"Then I am delighted to welcome you back, *Monsieur,*" the Proprietor replied.

Warren then ordered a bottle of champagne and made it clear that he required it to be served without delay.

As the Proprietor took the wine-list from him, Warren turned to look at the girl beside him and said with a smile:

"Now suppose we introduce ourselves? My name is Warren Wood."

There was a little pause before she replied:

"Mine is Nadia."

"Is that all?"

"Charrington."

"So you *are* English!"

Even as he spoke he was sure, again with a perception which was instinctive in him, that although her English seemed almost perfect, her appearance denied it.

There was nothing he could put his finger on, but he was certain there was some other nationality to which her blood owed allegiance.

Yet Warren thought it was a mistake to sound as if he was questioning anything she told him, and he said:

"Now we know each other, suppose you tell me what you are doing in Paris and why you are so anxious to leave it?"

As if she found the way he was expressing it almost amusing, he thought there was a slight smile on her lips before she replied:

"You promised we would talk . . . about you!"

"Very well, I will keep my word," Warren replied, "which incidentally, I always do."

He knew she would understand he was reassuring her that he would let her leave the moment she wished to go, and he had no other designs on her.

"I arrived," he continued, "in Paris to-night from Africa, and I am leaving first thing tomorrow morning for England."

"You have been in Africa? What have you been doing there?"

"I was travelling with a friend who is

writing a book on the tribes of North Africa, particularly the Berbers. We have been to places where they had never seen a white man before, and very nearly left our bones behind."

"It sounds very dangerous!"

"It was! At the same time, as I just told you, it cured me of wishing to kill myself."

She looked at him and he knew she was taking in the smartness of his evening-clothes and was aware of how expensive they were.

After a second she said:

"You do not look as though there was . . . any reason for you to want to . . . die."

"There are other reasons why people commit suicide besides lack of money!"

"Yes, I suppose there are," she agreed, "but being absolutely penniless and . . . alone is very . . . frightening!"

The way she said 'alone' made Warren lower his voice as he asked:

"Who have you lost?"

"M-my . . . mother."

"And you have no father?"

"My father is . . . dead."

There was a tremor on the last word which made Warren feel there was something particularly painful about the way she had lost her father.

"And you have no other relations who could look after you?"

"N-no . . . not in Paris."

It was quite obvious she had not the money to go anywhere else and he said:

"It seems impossible that anyone in this overcrowded city should be completely without friends, relatives or acquaintances."

She looked away from him as if she did not wish to reply, and he noticed her eyelashes were very long and dark.

After a moment he said lightly:

"Then perhaps I have been sent as your 'Guardian Angel' to save you from yourself."

"Which is something you . . . should not have done."

"Why not?"

She sighed.

"Because it is only . . . prolonging the agony."

There was no time for him to reply because the Proprietor brought the vichyssoise soup and set the bowls down in front of them.

They were accompanied by a basket containing crisp rolls warm from the oven, and there was a large pot of butter.

It was then that Warren knew how desperately hungry Nadia was, not because she rushed at the food, but because she deliberately waited, almost as if she was counting the seconds before her hand went out to touch the roll.

Slowly, so slowly that he knew she was forcing her will to behave with propriety she broke it, helped herself to the butter and spread a very small piece of the crust with it.

Then again she waited before she lifted it to her lips.

Warren pretended not to notice.

Instead he tasted the champagne, asked that there should be just a little poured into the glasses and the bottle then returned to the ice-cooler.

He also asked for a bottle of mineral water.

By the time all this was done Nadia was delicately and slowly drinking a spoonful of the soup.

As she did so, Warren thought, although it might have been his imagination, there was already just a touch more colour in the deathly whiteness of her skin.

She made no sound until the soup was finished.

Then, as she took a sip of the Evian water, Warren said:

"Try to drink a little champagne. It will give you an appetite."

"Do you think I need a stimulus to . . . acquire that?"

"I have learnt from experience," he replied, "that when one has been without food for a long time and you think you are very hungry, it is surprising that when the food is actually there you suddenly have no desire to eat it."

"Did you learn that in Africa?"

"Yes," he answered, "amongst a great many other things."

"I would like to hear about them."

"Are you really interested, or just pretending to be?"

For the first time she gave a little laugh.

"Actually I am interested, but I admit I have not thought about anything except my own troubles for what seems a long time."

"When did your mother die?"

He thought for a moment she would not reply. Then she said:

"Two days ago. She was . . . buried this morning."

Then, as if without his asking her she knew what he wanted to know, she added:

"I sold Mama's wedding-ring, her clothes, and everything I possessed to pay for the Funeral. Even so, the Priest had to help me from the Charity Funds."

She said the word 'charity' as if it was an insult, and Warren said:

"I understand. So you have nothing except for what you stand up in."

"M-must we . . . talk about it?"

"That is why we are here."

"Very well . . . you may as well know the truth. I have nothing, and nowhere to stay tonight. In the circumstances the river seems very inviting."

"As long as you end there, and not in some extremely uncomfortable prison."

She looked at him sharply before she replied:

"You seem very certain that I should be prevented from doing what I want to do. But every day dead bodies are discovered in the river, and no one has prevented them from drowning."

"You are one of the lucky — or unlucky — ones, whichever way you like to think about it."

"Unlucky? Of course I am unlucky!"

He was thinking of what he should say to her when the chicken arrived.

It was deliciously cooked with cream, and there were vegetables and sautéd potatoes to go with it.

As he had anticipated, Nadia could eat

only a very little, despite the fact that he noticed she took several little sips of her champagne.

Then she put down her knife and fork, looked at him pleadingly and said:

"Forgive me . . . when you have been so kind . . . but you are quite right . . . and it is impossible for me to . . . eat any more."

A waiter took away their plates and Warren ordered coffee and said:

"Now, suppose you tell me how you are in such a plight when it is obvious that you are educated, and are also what is called a 'Lady'?"

To his surprise Nadia stiffened and again looked away from him.

"I . . . I am not being rude," she said, "but . . . I cannot answer that question."

"Why not? I wish to understand."

She clasped her hands together and he knew that she felt she was being very obstructive before she said:

"It is a story I can tell . . . nobody . . . but Mama and I came to Paris because . . . if you like . . . we were in hiding . . . and our money gradually grew less and less. Then . . . Mama became ill."

"So you spent what you had on doctors' fees!"

Nadia nodded.

"But they were hopeless. They could do nothing for Mama and as she was in pain and I could not afford the right food . . . or the proper attention for her . . . it was perhaps a . . . good thing that she . . . died. I . . . I mean . . . good for her."

"I know what you are saying," Warren said sympathetically. "There is nothing worse than watching somebody you love suffer, and not being able to help."

He was thinking as he spoke of his father, and he could understand how frightening it had been for somebody like the girl beside him who was obviously wellborn.

"I wish you would tell me the whole story," he said.

She shook her head.

"I . . . I cannot do that. All I can say is: Thank you very much for giving me such a . . . delicious meal!"

She looked at him as if she expected him to get up and leave, and he replied:

"You are not so foolish as to think that I would walk away and leave you here. Even if I gave you some money, which I could quite easily do, I would not be able to sleep at night wondering what had happened to you."

He smiled before he added:

71

"I am sure you would feel the same. We all want to know the end of the story!"

"Perhaps there will not be one!"

"Nonsense! You are well aware that is not true! One chapter is finished, but life at your age and mine, I hope, will perhaps be more enjoyable in the next chapter than in the one which we have just completed."

Nadia's eyes seemed to fill her whole face as she said:

"What . . . can I do?"

It was the cry of a child who was afraid of the dark, and Warren answered:

"I have an idea which has suddenly come to me almost as if I heard it spoken by somebody outside myself, and yet I am almost afraid to tell you about it."

"There is no need for you to be that."

"Very well, I will risk your saying it is quite preposterous, and yet it is in my mind and I can see it falling into place like a jig-saw puzzle."

"You are making me . . . curious."

At the same time as she spoke Warren saw there was a wary look in her eyes, and he knew that she was afraid that his suggestion, proposition, or whatever it might be, was what she had feared in the first place.

Almost as if he could read her thoughts

he was aware that she was measuring the distance between her seat and the door.

If he said what she anticipated he might say, she could get up and run from the Restaurant and be down the road and out of sight before he could follow her.

"It is nothing like that," he said very quietly.

Now the wary look in her eyes changed to one of startled surprise because he had read her thoughts, and as he saw the colour come into her cheeks, it made her look surprisingly lovely.

chapter three

Choosing his words carefully, Warren said again:

"I arrived back in Paris tonight having been in Africa for nearly ten months during which time I have had no letters and seen no English newspapers."

He realised that Nadia was listening intently to what he said and continued:

"The reason why I went to Africa was that a woman to whom I was secretly engaged changed her mind because she found a man in a more advantageous social position than myself, and decided that a title was more important than love."

He was trying to speak in the same calm voice he had used all the evening, but now he remembered what he had felt when Magnolia had told him she preferred Raymond.

He was also furious at the deceitfulness

with which she was trying to get back into his life, and this changed his voice and, although he was not aware of it, the expression on his face.

"I was wondering when I went for a walk by the Seine," Warren went on, "how, when I return to England tomorrow I can avoid the scenes which I will undoubtedly have to endure from a woman who is incapable of speaking the truth."

Again the condemnation seemed almost to vibrate from his lips and he finished by saying:

"Now I have no wish to die, but instead I would find it very easy to commit murder!"

If he had intended to startle Nadia he certainly succeeded.

He saw her large eyes widen, and her fingers were clasped together as if she was personally disturbed at the violence of his words.

Then as if he remembered how young and frail she was, he said in a different tone:

"Forgive me, I should not speak like that, but I wanted you to understand and help me."

There was a little pause before she said:

"I would like to help you, but I cannot

see how it is . . . possible for me to . . . do so."

"When I walked by the Seine tonight," Warren answered, "my thoughts were of vengeance; how I could hurt somebody who had made me suffer so acutely that, like you, I wished to end my life."

There was silence as if he was feeling for words before he added:

"A dozen different ideas rushed through my mind, one of them being that I might hire an actress to return to England with me."

Nadia looked puzzled.

"Why should you wish to do that?"

"Because I thought the one certain way to show the woman of whom I am speaking I am no longer interested in her," Warren explained, "would be to come home with either a wife or a *fiancée*."

Now Nadia was very still as if she understood what he was saying to her.

Then as if she thought it was impossible for him to entertain such an idea she said:

"And you . . . intended to find this . . . actress?"

"It was just a wild idea which is impracticable because I am leaving tomorrow and have already telegraphed to my mother to expect me."

"Then . . . what are you . . . saying?"

Her words were very low, but he heard them.

"I am saying," he replied, "that it seems to be fate that you should come into my life at this particular moment, or should I say that once again our Guardian Angels have taken a hand in making things easier for both of us?"

"I . . . I still do not . . . understand."

"What I am suggesting is that you should come back to England with me as my *fiancée*. You will not come under your own name, so there will be no embarrassment for you as a person. We will give you a name and, to make my revenge really effective, a title!"

He almost spat the last words, then seeing Nadia draw in her breath he controlled himself to say without any expression in his voice:

"I will ask you to play your part for as long as it is necessary. Then we can announce to the few people who will be interested that we find we are incompatible, and I will pay you enough money to keep you in comfort for a long time. I will also try to find your Charrington relations who can look after you."

He paused and realised that Nadia was

staring at him as if she could not believe what she had heard.

Then as if she was convinced it was a fantasy she said:

"I . . . I suppose you are joking?"

"I have never been more serious."

"But it is . . . impossible! How could I do . . . such a thing?"

"Why not?"

"You have only just met me . . . you know . . . nothing about me."

"That is immaterial. What is important is that nobody in England knows anything about you. They will therefore accept exactly what we tell them."

"I would . . . make mistakes . . . I would let you . . . down!"

"I see no reason why you should do that. I think it would be a mistake for you to be English, and foreigners are not supposed to be *au fait* with all the protocol of English social life."

Nadia looked away from him, then quite unexpectedly she laughed.

"I do not believe . . . this is true!" she said. "I must be dreaming, or perhaps by mistake I am . . . acting in a very . . . strange Comedy."

"As far as I am concerned, it is a drama which might easily have become a tragedy."

Warren was frowning as he remembered how desperate he had been when Edward had joined him at the Club, and how agonising the wounds Magnolia had inflicted on him had been, for months after he left England.

It was only when the difficulties, problems and discomforts of everyday life in the desert had occupied him almost exclusively that she had ceased to haunt him.

He knew however that what she had made him suffer had left scars that would remain on his mind and what he thought of as his heart for the rest of his life.

As if while he was thinking Nadia was also turning over in her mind what he had told her, she said:

"Suppose when you see . . . this lady again you . . . realise that you . . . love her so much that you will . . . forgive her as she . . . wants you to do?"

"Never!"

As he spoke a surge of rage seemed to sweep over him and he brought his clenched fist down on the table, making the glasses jump.

"Never! Never!" he declared. "Let me make this quite clear, Nadia: I have finished with love, and if I do marry eventually because I want an heir, it will be a marriage of convenience such as the French have and which proves in most cases exceedingly successful."

The cynical lines on his face seemed to accentuate as he added:

" 'Once bitten, twice shy!' I will never allow myself to be humiliated again."

"I can understand your feelings," Nadia said. "At the same time perhaps, although you did not realise it, it is better to have learned what the lady was like . . . before she became your . . . wife rather than . . . afterwards."

This was something which had never occurred to Warren before, and he thought that Nadia certainly had a point.

He visualised, because he had a very fertile imagination, what he would have felt if after they had been married if he had to watch Magnolia yearning to be with Raymond instead of with him.

What was more, she could have been deeply envious that she could not live at Buckwood, or eventually become a Marchioness.

He would have tried to please her, tried to ensure that she was not discontented in the small house they would have lived in on the estate.

Yet he knew now as Nadia had suggested, it would have been a slow and painful agony to acknowledge the truth, and better to endure the short, sharp blow Magnolia had given him which had nearly knocked him out.

As if he could not bear to think of what might have been, he said abruptly:

"Let us concern ourselves with the situation as it is. Will you help me?"

"Do you really think I can?"

He looked at her and said:

"Shall I be very frank? You are a Lady. I know without your telling me that you are well-educated, and if you were properly fed and well-dressed you would be strikingly beautiful."

He spoke quite impersonally as if he were cataloguing Nadia's finer points, and yet the colour swept into her face, making her seem not only very young, but also very human.

Because she was so pale, so thin and so unhappy, she had seemed somewhat divorced from reality, but now she was only a young girl who had received a compliment.

Then she gave a little cry:

"You said: 'well-dressed'! I have already . . . told you that I possess . . . nothing! I have sold . . . everything . . . even my shoes."

"In which case we have to work very swiftly."

He drew his gold watch from his waistcoat pocket and looked at the time.

It was almost eleven-thirty.

He raised his hand to catch the Proprietor's attention who understood that he wanted his bill.

It was ready and as he put it down on the table Warren placed a large number of *francs* on the plate and rose to his feet.

"Come along!" he said, "we will find a *voiture* then I will tell you where we are going."

He knew as Nadia rose that she was still contemplating whether she would do as he suggested, or run off and find her way to the river without his interference.

Then as if something young and irrepressible within her told her that she would rather live than die, she gave him a faint smile.

They walked into the street and when they reached the main road that ran alongside the Seine they saw a *voiture* for hire coming towards them.

"Take us to the *Rue de Rivoli,* to the late market!" Warren ordered.

The cab-driver touched his hat with his whip and obviously impressed by Warren's appearance replied:

"*Bien, Monsieur!*"

Warren got in beside Nadia who asked:

"Why are we going there?"

"Because it is the only place open at this time of the night," Warren explained, "and I have to buy you a cape and perhaps a hat before I can take you into my *Hôtel.*"

She looked at him quickly, and he said:

"I am going to ask the Manager's wife, who I remember is a very able woman, to find you enough clothes in which you can travel to England. After that my mother will provide you with those that you lost while you were travelling to Paris."

"Will your mother believe that?"

"You must make certain she does. At the same time we have first to have a convincing story to tell *Madame* Blanc who, I am quite certain, will be very inquisitive."

He was silent as the *voiture* drove over a bridge of the Seine and a few minutes later they were in the *Rue de Rivoli.*

At the smart end where it joined the *Place de la Concorde* the shops at this late hour were of course all closed.

But Warren had remembered that beyond the Louvre, where there were the big, cheap Emporiums, there were also some small shops which stayed open late.

There was also an open market where one could buy food as well as all sorts of strange objects which the French considered bargains.

When the *voiture* came to a standstill Warren got out and told the man to wait.

Taking Nadia by the arm they mingled with the throng of ordinary people who had just come out from the Restaurants or the Theatres and a number of rag pickers who were doubtless also pick-pockets.

Warren steered Nadia through the crowd which was very good-humoured, joking and laughing amongst themselves, until he found a shop that was illuminated and its door still open.

There were a number of flashy gowns and some very seductive under-garments in the window, but inside there was a clothes' horse with a long rail on which there hung some long cloaks which the Parisian women wore at night over their evening-gowns.

He picked out one which was on a hanger but thought it too gaudy, then found another in a dark blue material that he placed over Nadia's shoulders.

It reached almost to the ground, concealing her threadbare gown, and he thought it suited her.

"You will have to choose the hat," he said.

He pointed to where there was a miscellaneous collection of hats: straws, velvets, some decorated with feathers or flowers, some gaudy, all heaped together on the side of a counter.

Nadia hesitated.

Then with what he thought was unerring good taste she picked out one that was plain and yet unmistakably had a touch of Paris *chic* about it.

It was a light felt, obviously left over from the winter collection, but it was small and trimmed only with one large black quill stuck into the band around the crown.

She put it on her head and looked at him for approval.

"Excellent!" he exclaimed.

He paid an indifferent saleswoman who looked tired and was obviously watching the clock for closing-time.

They walked back to the *voiture*, Warren gave the address of his *Hôtel* to the cab-driver, and as they set off up the *Rue de Rivoli* he said:

"Now you have another part to play, and I shall be interested to see how good an actress you are."

"You are . . . frightening me!"

"You certainly need not be frightened of *Madame* Blanc, although I admit I have found her somewhat intimidating in the past!"

Nadia realised he was laughing at her and she said:

"Please tell me quickly what I have to do."

"This part of the story is rather complicated," Warren said. "I left the *Hôtel* telling the Manager I had to leave first thing in the morning for England. He was to make all the arrangements for me. I return with a very beautiful young woman, for which the French have only one possible explanation!"

He did not wait for Nadia to reply to this but went on:

"I should have asked you this before, but what other languages do you speak besides English and French?"

He knew from Nadia's momentary hesitation that she was considering what reply to make.

It was strange how he could read her thoughts and was aware when he intruded on something she wished to keep a secret.

He did not even think it was extraordinary that he was so perceptive about her.

He only knew that his instinct told him so much more than she would put into words.

Hesitatingly she said:

"I . . . I can speak . . . Hungarian."

"Good! That is exactly what I hoped, or rather, that it would be the language of one of the Balkan countries of which most people are lamentably ignorant."

He smiled at her in the darkness of the *voiture* as he said:

"This will fit in with the tale we will tell when we reach England, so at least you need not change your identity."

"It sounds like something in a novel!" Nadia exclaimed.

"We have to make it credible!"

"Very well then . . . I am Hungarian."

"Tell me an Hungarian name."

"Ferrais, or Kaunitz!"

"Ferrais will do," he said, "and your father is an extremely wealthy nobleman."

Nadia did not speak and he continued:

"Because he is so wealthy you were kidnapped when you were travelling to Paris and held to ransom."

Warren spoke every word as if he was seeing it happening as he described it.

"The men who captured you were utterly and completely ruthless. They starved you, told your father you would die unless he paid them an enormous sum of money, confiscated your clothes, your jewellery, in fact, everything you possess."

"It sounds . . . terrifying!" Nadia exclaimed, but there was a hint of laughter in her voice.

"Then today, by some great good fortune," Warren went on, "I discovered among my letters an anonymous communication telling me where I would find you. Because your captors were not expecting you to be rescued, I was able to steal you away without their preventing me."

Nadia clapped her hands.

"It is exactly like one of the novelettes Mama would never let me read."

"Well, now you can not only read it but live it," Warren replied, "and make it convincing."

"To *Madame* Blanc?"

"Exactly! We are relying on her not only to believe you, but to provide you with the clothes in which you will travel to England, and in which you will look very attractive, despite all the privations you have suffered at the hands of your kidnappers."

"And you really think she will . . . believe us?"

"It depends on how well we tell the story!"

★ ★ ★

When several hours later Warren went to bed he stood for a moment at the window looking out over the moonlit view beneath him.

There was a smile of satisfaction on his lips which had not been there when he had looked at it before.

He had known, when he told his dramatic tale to *Monsieur* and *Madame* Blanc in the Manager's Office and saw their absorbed attention to what he was saying, that Nadia would not fail him either here in France, or when they reached England.

She played admirably the part of a shocked and frightened young girl who had suddenly been subjected to the horrors she had endured after being kidnapped.

Wisely, she said very little except to exclaim piteously over her sufferings.

Her thin face and huge eyes were so pathetic that he knew *Madame* Blanc's heart had been wrung with sympathy.

"Because I could not bring my cousin here to the *Hôtel* in the state to which she had been reduced," Warren explained, "I bought her a few clothes at the market in the *Rue de Rivoli*. But you understand, *Madame*, she must have something very different in which to travel to England."

89

"I can of course buy clothes very easily, *Monsieur*," *Madame* Blanc assured him, "but not until the shops are open, and *Mademoiselle la Comtesse* must have the best!"

"Yes, of course, the very best!" Warren agreed. "And money is no object."

He thought as he spoke of the huge fortune he would inherit when he became the head of the family in his uncle's place, and knew that for the first time in his life there was no need for him to count the cost of anything.

He made it clear to *Madame* Blanc that Nadia's father would reimburse him for anything he spent, so that it would be foolish to buy cheap things that they would throw away when they reached England.

"My cousin is used to having clothes that are the envy of all her friends," he said with a smile, "so I must look to you, *Madame,* to replace those which have been stolen from her."

"But of course, *Monsieur!*" *Madame* Blanc said eagerly.

Then she looked at her husband.

"How long do I have, Etienne, before *Monsieur* wishes to depart?"

It took quite a lot of argument and pleading from *Madame* before Warren finally condescended to leave Paris on a later train which would connect not with the morning Cross-Channel Steamer from Calais but the afternoon boat.

This would mean their arriving much later, but he knew it was impossible for him to take Nadia to England without the right clothes.

He had no wish to tell the kidnapping story to his mother, or to anybody else the other side of the Channel.

That story was for French consumption only, and in England he intended to say that he had met Nadia in Paris *en route* to Africa, that he had fallen in love with her and she had waited for his return to Paris before they announced their engagement formally.

He felt this was a safe story considering that nobody except Edward knew how long they had stayed in Paris before they went to Africa and there was no reason why Nadia should not have met him at Marseilles on his homeward journey.

This would mean that he would not have read his mother's letter, or for that matter, Magnolia's, until he arrived in Paris.

It all seemed to fit in very well, and he knew, if he was honest, that he rather enjoyed that intrigue and working out the plot he had invented himself, although

Nadia was very important in it.

After they had talked for a long time in the Manager's Office he realised she was looking tired and suggested to *Madame* Blanc that Nadia should go to bed.

"I am sure, *Madame*," he said in his most charming manner which was difficult for any woman to resist, "you will look after my cousin tonight and chaperon her very effectively. Tomorrow, I intend to take her to my mother's who will be horrified at what has occurred."

"I am sure that is true, *Monsieur*," *Madame* Blanc replied, "and *Mademoiselle* can sleep in the room next to mine because my daughter who usually occupies it is staying with friends."

"I am very grateful, *Madame*."

Madame Blanc bustled Nadia upstairs, gave her a hot drink to help her sleep, and helped her to undress.

She exclaimed in horror at the condition of the gown which was all her captors had given her to wear!

She promised that tomorrow she should have the most beautiful gowns that Paris could provide, besides mantals, hats, gloves and everything else that could be bought at a moment's notice.

"What I intend to do, *Mademoiselle la*

Comtesse," *Madame* Blanc said in her firm, practical voice, "is to set off at dawn without you to find what is available in your size. You are very slim, so it should not be difficult. Then later, when you have had *petit déjeuner* one of my staff will bring you to join me and see if you approve of my taste."

"I am sure, *Madame,* that anything you select for me will be delightful and very *chic!*" Nadia replied.

She knew by the smile on *Madame*'s face that no Frenchwoman could resist the chance of spending unlimited money, even if it was for another woman!

Nadia was in fact exhausted, and almost as soon as her head touched the pillow she fell asleep.

Madame Blanc then returned to her husband's Office where he and Warren were still talking.

"*La pauvre petite est très fatiguée!*" she commented.

"I only hope the journey tomorrow will not be too much for her," Warren said, "but I have to go home."

"I thought perhaps the urgency concerned your family," *Madame* Blanc said, "but I did not like to mention it before."

"What do you mcan?"

In answer the Manager handed him from his desk a copy of *Le Temps* and pointed to a paragraph low on the front page.

It was almost what Warren had expected as he translated:

"DEATH OF A DISTINGUISHED ENGLISH NOBLEMAN

It is with deep regret that we learn today of the death of the Marquis of Buckwood at his home in Oxfordshire . . ."

The newspaper went on to describe the Marquis's importance at Court, his vast possessions, his visit to France at the opening of the Exhibition and finished:

"The Marquis's only son died very recently after a riding accident. The heir to the title is his nephew Mr. Warren Wood, who has been abroad for some months and is not aware of his new position.

Every effort is being made by the Solicitors to the estate to get in touch with Mr. Wood."

Warren finished reading the account and

as he put down the newspaper the Manager said:

"My condolences, *Monsieur,* and also my congratulations!"

"Thank you," Warren replied. "Now you understand why I must go home as quickly as possible."

"Of course, *Monsieur,* but as *Madame* has said, clothes cannot be purchased until the shops are open."

"No, of course not," Warren replied, "and clothes even in these circumstances are very important."

Then *Madame* exclaimed:

"You do not intend, *Monsieur,* that I should buy everything in black for *Mademoiselle la Comtesse?*"

Warren thought quickly, remembering that Nadia was in mourning for her mother.

At the same time it would spoil his return with her if she was, as Magnolia had been, restricted by the strict protocol of mourning.

He shook his head.

"No, there is no need for *Mademoiselle* to be in mourning," he replied. "Our relationship is through my mother's family, and there is therefore no reason why she should be affected in that way by my uncle's death."

"I am glad!" *Madame* Blanc exclaimed. "Mourning makes us all, as I have said before to my husband, look like a lot of black crows!"

Warren smiled.

He knew if any country in the world could make mourning look attractive and even seductive, it was France.

The little touches of white on a black gown, the transparency of chiffon or lace over the skin, were very different from the heavy crêpe, the profusion of jet, and the gloom of British black.

He merely said aloud:

"I suggest, *Madame,* that you make my relative look as young and as beautiful as she was before she suffered so acutely at the hands of those villains."

"I hope, *Monsieur,* they will receive their just deserts!"

"Her father the Count will certainly see to that," Warren replied. "But it is best for us to get out of the country before anything untoward happens. Such men if thwarted in their desire for money, can be very dangerous!"

"That is true, *Monsieur,*" *Madame* Blanc agreed. "So you must certainly catch the second Express as my husband has suggested."

"Everything will be arranged, *Monsieur*," the Manager said, "a private compartment in the train, the best cabin on the Steamer, and a Courier to travel with you who will see to everything."

"Thank you!" Warren replied.

He thought now as he stood at the window that it was almost amusing.

Suddenly as if by a magic wand, his whole life had changed.

From now on there would be Couriers, valets, footmen, to run at his bidding, and waiting for him in England would be Secretaries, Managers and Agents who had helped his uncle run the estates.

They saw to it that each one of his houses functioned like a well-oiled machine with no breakdowns and no problems to cause his sleepless nights.

'I am lucky, unbelievably lucky!' he thought.

He drew the curtains to shut out the moonlight and got into bed.

Sitting beside Nadia in the reserved carriage on the Boat Train carrying them from Dover to London, Warren thought she looked if a little tired, exceedingly lovely.

He knew she had slept in the comfortable cabin that had been engaged for them for the Channel crossing.

He on the other hand, had walked the decks feeling he needed the fresh air, and finding the smooth sea and the last rays of the afternoon sun delightful.

He appreciated, although he did not say so, every luxury they had enjoyed so far, not only because it was so very different from the discomforts of Africa, but also because he knew it was prophetic of his whole future.

He had waited until now to tell Nadia his new name and title, although he had noticed she was astute enough to look puzzled when the Manager addressed him as: *'Milord'* rather than *'Monsieur.'*

"When you had gone to bed last night," Warren said to her, "the Manager showed me a copy of *Le Temps* in which there was a report of my uncle's death."

"I am sorry if it has upset you."

"It was what I expected," Warren said, "because my mother had warned me. After his son was killed he had a heart-attack and was in a coma. This means that I am now the sixth Marquis of Buckwood!"

Nadia did not speak for a moment. Then she asked:

"Does that make you feel very important?"

"Yes, very!" he replied. "Especially as I never anticipated for one moment that I would ever inherit such a position!"

"Then I am glad for you, but it will make the lady who wishes to marry you very angry!"

"Very angry indeed!" Warren said with satisfaction.

Then as if he had no wish to talk about himself he added:

"We must go over our story to be quite certain before we arrive that you are word-perfect."

"I am so afraid of making mistakes . . . then you will be . . . angry."

"I promise you I shall not be that," he said. "And after the splendid way in which you carried off our fantastic tale last night, I am sure there is a fortune waiting for you on the stage at Drury Lane!"

She laughed as if that was such an impossibility that it was but a figment of his imagination.

Then Warren said:

"Judging from the amount of luggage which you now possess, I imagine there is no hurry for us to visit any English shops, and you can cope at any rate for a few weeks in the country."

"I am afraid *Madame* Blanc has spent a

great amount of money," Nadia said.

"That is immaterial beside the fact that you have to look right for the part."

"I should certainly do that," Nadia said in a low voice. "I have never seen such wonderful gowns, nor did I imagine it was possible to buy so much so very quickly!"

She gave a little laugh before she said:

"I really believe *Madame* was up all night hammering on the doors of the dress-makers. In fact she told me that at one shop the seamstresses had been paid extra to go to work at four o'clock in the morning because they had a special wedding-gown to finish."

Warren laughed.

"They cannot have been very pleased to see another customer!"

"According to *Madame* they were delighted, and actually that particular bride will have three of her gowns delivered late!"

Warren laughed again.

"If there is one thing the French are really adept at, it is the turning of any emergency to their own advantage! I am certain the gowns that were switched cost double in the process, but were well worth the expense!"

"I only hope you will think so," Nadia

said, "and I am very embarrassed at costing you so much."

"I would pay a hundred times more to be sure of creating the effect I want."

The hard, bitter note was back in his voice and Nadia looked at him apprehensively.

Quickly, because she thought the violence of his emotions spoilt him, she talked of other things, asking him further about the history of Buckwood and to explain the members of the family whom she would meet.

Because she seemed to have grasped so quickly the different relationships and even the different titles she would encounter in the family tree, Warren, as he talked, was quite certain that it was not new ground to her, but something she was familiar with in her own life.

The more he was with her, the more he looked at her, the more he was certain she was blue-blooded to her finger-tips.

Although she would tell him nothing more about herself, he was aware of a mystery which intrigued and fascinated him and he knew he would never rest until he had learnt her whole secret.

At the same time, he knew it would be a great mistake to upset her in any way, or for her to resent his prying into things which did not concern him.

All that mattered at the moment was that everybody should be convinced that he was intending to marry somebody with whom he was not only deeply in love, but who was also eminently suited to become the Marchioness of Buckwood.

"I was wondering," he said aloud, "whether I should make you a Princess, but I think that might be dangerous because there must be Hungarians in England who would at least know those in their country who were of Royal blood."

"That is true," Nadia said seriously, "and as almost everybody one meets in Hungary is a Count that would be very much safer."

Warren was aware that if a Count had even a dozen children they all inherited his title, each one of them becoming a Count or a Countess, unlike in England where the title went only to the eldest son.

As if she wished to please him, Nadia said:

"There is however no reason why my mother should not have a little Royal blood in her, if you wish to improve the story."

"That sounds a good idea," Warren said.

"There are on the Russian border," Nadia said hesitatingly, "quite a number of families who consider themselves . . . Royal . . . although they play no part . . . in the governing of the country."

"I am aware of that," Warren smiled, "and it is clever of you, Nadia, to suggest that your mother should be Royal. I imagine you can give me the name of some large family to which she could quite easily belong."

"Of course," Nadia replied. "There are so many Rákócitz that I doubt if anybody but a Hungarian could count them all!"

"Very well, your mother was a Princess of the family, and you had better give me her Christian name."

"Shall we say Olga?"

"Excellent!" Warren said. "Princess Olga! And as the daughter of a great land-owner, Count Viktor Ferrais, you are of course, by no means overawed by or in any way subservient to the Marquis of Buckwood!"

"Of course not," Nadia agreed her eyes twinkling. "In fact, I am only afraid that my family will not think him good enough for me!"

They both laughed and Warren told himself that he was certainly in luck when he had seen a slim figure looking down into the dark waters of the Seine and realised what she was about to do.

It was however a little after midnight when finally they reached his mother's house, and Nadia was very tired.

On Warren's instructions telegrams had been sent before he went to bed the night before to his mother and to his uncle's secretary at Buckwood House in London and, as he expected, there were carriages to meet them at Victoria Station.

They were carried swiftly across London to where it seemed almost as if at his command the train was waiting to convey them to the nearest station to Buckwood.

More carriages, more servants, and at last they walked into his mother's house to find her waiting for him, her arms outstretched.

"You should be in bed, Mama!" Warren said as he kissed her. "You should not have waited up for me."

"I could not rest until you were safely home," his mother replied. "Oh, dearest boy, I am so delighted to see you!"

She kissed him again before she looked curiously at Nadia.

"Mama," Warren said slowly and impressively, "may I introduce the Countess

Nadia Ferrais, who has come with me and who I am very proud to tell you has promised to become my wife!"

He knew what he had said was a shock to his mother, but as he expected, she took it with her usual gracious dignity saying:

"My dearest, I hope you will be very happy!"

Taking Nadia's hand in hers she said:

"I am very glad I shall have a daughter-in-law who will look after my son, and whom I know I shall love."

She spoke so gently and movingly that Warren saw the tears come into Nadia's eyes and knew she was thinking of her own mother.

Quickly, in case she should become emotional, he started to talk to his mother of how they had met when he was on his way to Africa, and how they had known they were meant for each other.

He told her how she was waiting for him when he arrived with Edward at Marseilles.

"She of course had one of her elderly relatives with her," he said, having just thought of it, "and although I begged her to come with us to England, she unfortunately had to return home to Hungary."

"I thought from your name you must be Hungarian," his mother said to Nadia, "and of course like all your countrywomen you are very beautiful, my dear!"

"Thank you," Nadia replied.

"She is also very tired," Warren interposed, "and I suggest, Mama, that she goes to bed immediately, and we can tell you everything about ourselves tomorrow."

"Yes, of course, dear boy."

His mother took Nadia upstairs to hand her over to an elderly maid who helped her into bed, and only after she herself also had retired did Warren go into her room to sit down beside her.

"I am so glad you are back in time for the Funeral," his mother said. "That you are engaged to be married will be cheerful news for the family, after they have been stricken first by Raymond's death, and now by poor Arthur's."

"I could hardly believe it was true when I read your letter," Warren said.

"It seems unbelievable," his mother agreed, "but dearest, first thing in the morning you must take charge of everything as they are expecting you to do."

"Of course, Mama!"

He rose to his feet as he spoke and added:

"Now I am going to bed for I too am tired. I seem to have been travelling for a very long time."

"You look very well, and I rather like the new colour of your skin."

"You mean my sun-tan? At times in the last few months I have been as dark as any Arab could be!"

"You look very handsome, as I am sure that charming young lady you have brought with you has told you already."

"She has been very ill, and is rather shy, Mama."

"She looks very young, and very sweet!" his mother replied.

She spoke with a note in her voice which made Warren know she was entirely sincere.

After a little pause she went on:

"You may be surprised to learn that Magnolia Keane is staying at Buckwood!"

Warren started.

"Staying at Buckwood? Why should she do that?"

"She moved in with an elderly cousin whom she calls her chaperon after Raymond's accident. She appeared — then — to be overcome with sorrow. But your uncle's secretary, Mr. Greyshott, tells me she asked him searching questions about you and made it very clear that she wanted to get in touch with you."

"She has not come here, Mama?"

"Not since I refused to see her after you had left England."

"She tried to see you then?"

"I think after she learned you had gone away she was curious enough to want to know what had happened. Anyway, she called here and asked to see me, and I sent a message to say I was not well enough to receive strangers!"

Warren thought that his mother, when it suited her, could put down very cleverly, somebody who was pretentious or pushing but aloud he said:

"You will understand, Mama, that I have no wish to see Magnolia again. Although I had no chance of talking to you about it, the reason why I left England was that she told me she intended to marry Raymond."

"I knew that," his mother replied.

"How did you know it?" Warren asked curiously.

"Oh, my dear, I am not so stupid as not to be able to put two and two together! Moreover, although it is very regrettable, servants talk and nothing one can do will stop them!"

Warren drew in his breath.

"Do you mean to say that the servants at Buckwood realised that Magnolia was trying to capture Raymond while she was secretly engaged to me?"

"That is so, dear," his mother said, "and I can understand it makes you feel bitter about her. Personally, if you want the truth, I never liked Magnolia, nor did I trust her!"

"Then you were far more astute than I was!"

"Of course!" his mother agreed. "Women always find it very hard to deceive other women, and although, darling boy, so many women have loved you for yourself, I was always suspicious that where Magnolia was concerned, she put your background first and you second!"

Warren sighed.

"You make me feel very foolish, Mama, and in a way ashamed of myself."

"There is no need for you to be that," his mother said. "But I am thanking God that you have found somebody whom you can love and who will be marrying you, rather than your Family Tree!"

Warren laughed and it was quite a natural sound.

"Nadia assures me," he said, "that ours is quite a young sapling compared to her father's."

"I would not be at all surprised," his mother replied, "for the Hungarians are a very proud people. Anyway, my dearest, I wish you every happiness which I have the unmistakable feeling is what you have found this time."

Only when he was in bed did Warren wonder if it was very reprehensible of him to start his new life by acting out a lie and deceiving somebody who trusted him as his mother did.

Then he told himself that at least Nadia provided him with an excuse for turning Magnolia immediately out of Buckwood and it would give him great pleasure to do so.

"Damn her!" he muttered. "How does she dare to come here, forcing herself upon the family as if she was Raymond's wife, and at the same time writing to me as she did?"

He knew as he asked himself the question that it would be a mistake to underrate Magnolia. She would fight desperately and in the most underhand and devious manner possible to get her own way.

"There is no reason why I should be afraid to take her on," Warren told himself.

At the same time he was not sure.

chapter four

Warren was having breakfast at seven-thirty the next morning when Mr. Greyshott came into the room.

He had been his uncle's chief Secretary ever since Warren could remember and was a grey-haired man of over fifty.

He was exceedingly efficient and had the character to exercise an authority which nobody disputed.

He had been at the station last night to meet Warren who now looked up with a smile to say:

"Good-morning, Greyshott! Despite the late hour at which I got to bed I am ready for all the burdens with which you no doubt propose to confront me!" Mr. Greyshott laughed and replied:

"I hope they will not be too over-whelming, My Lord."

"Sit down and tell me about the arrangements for tomorrow," Warren said in a different tone.

Mr. Greyshott sat down at the table and waved away the suggestion of coffee which the Butler offered him.

Then as the servants left the room Warren said:

"First I would like to know who is staying in the house and how many more you are expecting tonight."

"I thought Your Lordship would ask that," Mr. Greyshott answered, "and I am afraid it is a very long list. I had no idea until your cousin's funeral that so many Woods existed!"

"I have always known ours was a very large family," Warren replied, "but a great number of them did not concern me until now."

Mr. Greyshott handed him the list on which he saw the names of great-uncles, great-aunts, uncles, aunts, and innumerable cousins, besides close friends who had already arrived to be present at the Marquis's Funeral.

"I should think if they all stay with us the house will burst at the seams!" Warren remarked.

"We can manage," Mr. Greyshott replied reassuringly, "and I think, if you will permit me to say so, they will expect Your Lordship to move into the Master Suite to-night."

Warren accepted this because it was traditional and merely said:

"That is what I will do."

He was still reading the list as he spoke. Then at the bottom of it he found the names he was looking for.

"Miss Magnolia Keane"
"Mrs. Douglas Keane"

He looked up and chose his words with care as he said:

"I see no reason for Miss Keane to be staying in the house, and I suggest that if she wishes to attend the Funeral, which we cannot prevent her from doing, she should move to an *Hôtel* or to friends in the neighbourhood!"

His voice sharpened as he spoke, and as Mr. Greyshott did not reply he went on:

"As I expect you are aware, I have brought my fiancée with me, intending to announce my engagement formally. As things are, we shall have to wait a little while, but I would like you, Greyshott, to make it clear to the family why she is here."

He thought Mr. Greyshott looked at him in surprise and he added:

"It will be a little difficult for me in the circumstances, and it would be better if it came from you."

"Very well, if that is what you wish," Mr. Greyshott argued, "but I think, if you will forgive my saying so, My Lord, that it would be a mistake to turn Miss Keane out."

"Why?"

"Because she would certainly resent it, and she is getting a great deal of sympathy because, although it was supposed to be a secret, everybody knew at your cousin's Funeral that they were engaged."

Warren's lips tightened. Then he asked curiously:

"I cannot understand why their engagement had not been announced! After all, it would have been quite correct to have done so in March or April."

"That was what she wanted," Mr. Greyshott replied, "but your uncle insisted that there should be no formal announcement until Christmas."

Now Warren was surprised and raising his eyebrows asked:

"Why did he insist on that?"

Mr. Greyshott hesitated, and Warren said sharply:

"Tell me the truth, Greyshott. I want to know!"

"I think His Lordship did not like Miss Keane and was aware that when you brought her to stay with your mother you intended to marry her."

Warren was astonished.

"How could Uncle Arthur know that?"

"No one can stop servants talking," Mr. Greyshott said quietly, "and your uncle was very fond of you. In fact I think it would be true to say that he often wished you were his son rather than his nephew."

"In consequence he disliked Magnolia!" Warren said beneath his breath.

"I know that she pleaded with him and so did Raymond over the announcement of their engagement, but your Uncle was adamant. He told them that if they were both of the same mind at Christmas or perhaps at the time of the Hunt Ball at the beginning of December, their engagement could be announced then."

Warren knew that his uncle could be very dictatorial when it suited him, and he could understand Magnolia's frustration.

Then when Raymond was killed she realised all too clearly that she had lost the substance for the shadow.

There was a hard look in his eyes and a cynical twist to his lips as he said:

"All the same she has no part in Buckwood now, and the sooner you get rid of her the better!"

He knew by the expression on Mr. Greyshott's face that it was not going to be easy, and he asked sharply:

"Raymond did not make a will in her favour, or anything like that?"

"I understand she asked him to do so," Mr. Greyshott answered, "but your Uncle heard about it from the family Solicitors, and forbade Raymond to do anything of the sort."

Because he disliked everything he had heard he rose from the desk and said:

"I have no wish to see her, Greyshott. Tell her that I am here with my fiancée and will need the rooms she and Mrs. Keane are occupying."

"I will do that," Mr. Greyshott agreed.

At the same time, Warren knew he felt anxious.

There was a horse waiting for him at the door, and Warren rode across the fields to the big house.

As he saw it looking magnificent in the distance, with the Marquis's standard flying at half-mast, he thought it must be a dream that it now belonged to him.

The sunshine turned the hundreds of windows to gold and glittered on the lake and it seemed to Warren as if it had stepped out of a fairy-story.

He loved Buckwood as it had always been so much a part of his childhood and the memories of his father.

He knew that now he had come home he must devote himself to serving the house and the family traditions as his ancestors had done before him.

As he reached the front door he found there were several carriages outside.

He knew that the moment he entered the huge marble Hall with its statues of gods and goddesses and the flags com-memorating battles in which members of the family had fought valiantly, there would be the chatter of voices.

Whatever happened either in joy or sorrow, the Woods always made Buckwood a meeting place, where they could get to-gether and talk about themselves.

He was not mistaken.

He could hear their voices in the Drawing-Room as he entered the hall and saw the row of top-hats laid out on the table beneath the staircase.

Then with a faint smile because it was all

so familiar, he opened the door and joined them.

It was nearly an hour later when he extricated himself from the clinging arms of his female relations who had always been eager to kiss him because he was so handsome, and the hearty hand-shakes of the male representatives of the family.

It warmed his heart to realise that they were all genuinely glad that he should take his uncle's place as head of the family.

They had loved his father, for nobody ever managed to quarrel with Lord John, and in consequence they had adored and spoiled Warren ever since his birth.

It was only as he moved towards the Study where his uncle had always dealt with any business which affected the estate that he realised they had not yet learnt of his engagement and wondered what they would think of Nadia.

He had made it clear to the servants at his mother's house that she was to be allowed to sleep until she woke.

He decided that she should not attend the Funeral, although she would be expected to have luncheon and to dine with the family today when she would be introduced to them as his future wife.

He thought it would undoubtedly surprise them, but not so much as it would surprise Magnolia.

Mr. Greyshott was waiting for him in the Study.

He put down in front of him the arrangements for the Funeral, a copy of the Service which had already been printed with a wide black band on the outside cover, and a list of the guests at luncheon.

"The rest of the family will be arriving this afternoon," Mr. Greyshott explained, "and I will let you have the seating for dinner later on."

"Have you spoken to Miss Keane?"

"Yes, I have," he replied, "but she refuses to leave until she has seen you."

"I have no wish . . ." Warren began.

At that moment the door opened and Magnolia came into the Study.

A quick glance told Warren that she was even more beautiful than when he had last seen her.

He knew however as she moved towards him with a sensuous grace that somehow made the plain black gown she was wearing seem almost immorally seductive, that his only feeling for her was one of hatred.

With a murmured apology Mr. Greyshott moved quickly from the room.

As the door closed behind him Magnolia said in the soft, caressing voice that Warren remembered so well:

"You are back! Oh darling, it seems an eternity since I last saw you!"

He had risen to his feet when she appeared, but he had remained behind his desk and he replied coldly:

"I am surprised to find you here!"

"If I had left immediately after Raymond's funeral, I might have missed you. Did you not receive my letter in Paris?"

"I received your letter which arrived three days before I did!"

He knew as he spoke this was something she had not expected he would know and her long eye-lashes flickered.

At the same time she was quick-witted enough to say after just a faint pause:

"I wrote it soon after you left, but there was no point in sending it until I knew you were on your way home."

"Which, most conveniently, was after Raymond had his accident!"

Magnolia made a little gesture with her hands which was very expressive. Then she asked:

"Why are you talking to me like this? I told you I loved you, Warren, and I have always loved you. Surely you can forgive

120

me a moment's madness?"

She gave a deep sigh.

"When I saw this house I thought it was so beautiful that I could think of nothing except living in it and feeling as if I belonged . . ."

She spoke very softly and as if, Warren thought, she was trying to weave a spell around him from which he would find it hard to extract himself.

Then in a hard voice he interrupted her to say:

"It is no use, Magnolia! I am not prepared to stand here and listen to your lies! I told Mr. Greyshott to ask you to leave and that is what you have to do."

"He also told me you had brought your fiancée with you," Magnolia said. "Is that true?"

"Greyshott invariably tells the truth, as I do!"

"And you really intend to marry somebody other than — me?"

She asked the question mockingly and there was a laughing note in her voice.

Then deliberately, so that she took him by surprise, she moved round the desk and was standing close beside him.

She threw back her head to look up at him in a way he had always found irresistible and her lips were near to his as she whispered:

"Warren! Warren! I love you, as you love me. How could either of us forget the wonder and the glory we found when you kissed me?"

Then before Warren could move she pulled his head down to hers and her lips were on his.

He could feel the passion on them, could feel too the softness of her body against him and smell the seductive fragrance of her perfume that had something exotic about it.

But as she kissed him, her lips moving sensuously against his, he knew that her power over him had disappeared.

This contact with her dismissed the last lingering doubt in his mind whether she still had some hold over him.

His fingers closed over her wrists and he removed her arms from his neck.

"It is no use, Magnolia."

As she realised he was completely unmoved by her, he saw an expression first of incredulity in her dark eyes, then it was replaced by one of frustration and anger.

For a moment there was only silence, as if she found it hard to believe what he had said. Then she asked:

"Are you really sending me away?"

"I insist upon your leaving my house! While you are here it is only an embarrassment, and as your engagement to Raymond was not announced you have no official standing."

He released her wrists as he spoke and she rubbed one of them with her other hand as if he had hurt her.

"I believed that you — loved me."

"I did love you," Warren answered. "I loved you completely and whole-heartedly until I learnt that you were merely using me to serve your social ambition and were not interested in me as a man!"

"That is not true!" Magnolia cried. "And I love you now as I have never loved you before!"

"Only because you have lost me!" Warren replied cynically. "And you do not like being a loser."

"Have I really lost you?"

Now her voice was very soft and beguiling and he knew she was making one last desperate effort.

"As you already know, I am engaged to be married to somebody I love, a woman I can trust!"

Again his voice was sharp. Then he added:

"Goodbye, Magnolia. As you will understand, as I have a great deal of work to do, so I hope you will excuse me if I do not come to see you off."

He spoke with a formal politeness that was more shattering than if he had raged at her.

Magnolia walked slowly to the door and only as she reached it did she turn back to say:

"You will be sorry, Warren, that you treated me like this! And do not think that you can forget me so easily or find another woman who will excite you as I was always able to do!"

She paused before she went on in a voice that seemed to vibrate towards him:

"When you are kissing your *fiancée* you will remember my kisses. When you touch her skin it will not feel like mine. You will miss the beating of my heart and the sound of my voice telling you of my love!"

Now the tone of her voice was hypnotic, mesmeric, but as Warren listened he knew it was a very skilful performance and that the audience to whom it was addressed was not himself, but the Marquis of Buckwood.

"Goodbye, Magnolia!" he said sharply and sat down at his desk.

She lingered for a moment longer, then she was gone.

Only when he was certain she would not return did he rise to walk across the room to the open window.

He felt he needed fresh air.

He felt too as if he had been fighting against something which threatened to envelop him against his will and if he was not careful would destroy him.

Then he told himself he was being as theatrical as Magnolia had been, and the sooner he got back to sanity the better.

At the same time, he felt almost as if his collar was strangling him and it was hard to breathe.

Nadia came downstairs a little after eleven o'clock feeling ashamed that she had slept so late.

The Butler met her in the hall to say:

"Her Ladyship has asked me to apologise, M'Lady, and to inform you that as she was very fatigued through being up so late last night she will not be down until luncheontime."

"I quite understand," Nadia replied, "and I am late too."

"That was to be expected, M'Lady," the Butler said. "It's a very tiring journey from

Paris, I understand."

"Yes, very," Nadia agreed.

He opened the door of the Drawing-Room which had long French windows opening out into the garden.

Outside Nadia could see there was a formal rose-garden and because it was summer the roses were all in bloom, crimson, white, yellow, pink and gold, they made a lovely picture.

Everything was very quiet, except for the humming of the bees buzzing over the blossoms, and the birds singing in the bushes.

It was like stepping into a fairy-land after being condemned to the squalid bedroom which she and her mother had occupied on the Left Bank of the Seine.

Even to think of it after her mother had grown so ill made Nadia shudder.

A breakfast-tray had been brought to her bedside after she woke and as she had looked at the beautiful china, the silver cover which kept the eggs hot and the fine linen napkin embroidered with Lord John's monogram she wanted to cry.

How could her mother have endured the cheap, badly cooked food, served on cracked plates in their dirty, dilapidated attic?

It was not surprising, Nadia thought, that she had died not only of her illness, but also of starvation because it was impossible to provide her with the right nourishment.

"Oh, Mama, if only you were here now!" she cried out in her heart.

Then she knew it was no use grieving over the past and instead she had to think of the future.

"I am so lucky, so very, very lucky," she told herself, just as Warren had done.

She was thinking that if he had not saved her she would by now be buried in a pauper's grave and because she had committed suicide, without the prayers or the blessing of the Church.

At least her mother had had that.

Because she was aware how desperately tired she had felt last night and almost on the point of collapse, she forced herself to eat everything on the breakfast-tray even though it was a great effort.

"If I am to help him as he wishes me to do," she reasoned, "I have to be strong and, what is more, I must have my wits about me!"

Last night when the maid had been helping her undress, the woman's voice kept fading away and she felt as if she was moving in a fog.

Now everything was clear, but it was inevitable that the weeks — or was it months? — of misery and privation overshadowed with fear had taken their toll mentally and physically.

Now she was in England, her fear had receded into the background, and with her new identity, even though it was just play-acting, she need think of nothing except getting herself well and trying to do what kind Mr. Wood asked of her.

Then she remembered he was now a Marquis and wanted to laugh because it all seemed so incredible.

How could she have imagined for one moment when she went down to the Seine to drown herself that so soon she would find herself living in the luxury of an English mansion, waited on by attentive servants, such as she remembered in the past?

And knowing that hanging in the wardrobe were expensive, elegant gowns such as she had never expected to see again, let alone own?

"It is not true! I am dreaming!" Nadia exclaimed.

But because it was so exciting, she wanted to get up and see everything and do everything in case she woke up . . .

The sunshine in the garden, the roses, the red-brick wall enclosing them which she knew was very old and mellowed with age all seemed again part of her dreams.

Her mother had often described to her what an English garden was like.

Although she had never seen one, she knew now this was exactly what she had expected.

It was all so beautiful and there was no need to look over her shoulder or fear that somebody was approaching her, of lowering her voice in case what she was saying should he overheard.

"I am in England and I am safe!" she said aloud.

Because the sun was very hot she turned and walked back through the French windows into the Drawing-Room.

This again was exactly as her mother had described it to her; the comfortable sofas and armchairs, the tables on which there were innumerable and fascinating *objets d'art,* snuff-boxes, pieces of Dresden china, silver photograph frames with photographs of beautiful women which they had signed boldly and proudly.

There were portraits on the walls too, which were, Nadia thought, what she might have expected.

There was a beautiful painting by Sir Joshua Reynolds over the marble mantelpiece and a very attractive Greuze on one wall.

There was a 'Conversation Piece' of a family wearing the clothes of the previous century with a magnificent house in the background that she was sure was Buckwood.

It had been too dark last night to see the big house, and she hoped that Warren would show it to her today.

She already knew how much it meant to him. His voice had softened when he spoke of it and she had the feeling that it was as dear as the woman he had loved.

When she thought about him, seeing how handsome and attractive he was and, as she had found, kind and understanding, it seemed impossible that any woman should have thrown him over so cruelly that he now wished to have his revenge.

Nadia was far too perceptive not to be aware that the woman who had jilted Warren had made him suffer in a manner which he would never forget.

At the same time, she thought to herself, his bitterness was a flaw and seemed unworthy of him.

It was as if, she thought, looking across

the room, somebody had deliberately damaged the beautiful 'Conversation Piece' that she realised now had been painted by Gainsborough.

Then as she was looking at it, thinking that one day Warren should be painted in the same way together with his family and the house he loved behind him, the door of the Drawing-Room opened.

Nadia turned her head hoping it was Warren.

Instead she saw a woman who was so beautiful and so different from anybody she had seen before that she could only stare at her.

She was dressed in black which seemed to reveal every curve of her breasts and hips, and somehow made her seem theatrical as if she was on a stage.

There were two long strings of pearls round her neck and her hat was trimmed with black ostrich feathers.

Beneath it her skin was dazzlingly white and had the same translucence as her pearls.

Her eyes were dark, liquid, and fringed with long lashes.

She came gracefully across the room as Nadia watched, spellbound by her appearancc.

Then as she reached her the woman exclaimed:

"I understand you are trying to marry Warren!"

The rude way she spoke and her form of words was so surprising that for a moment Nadia could not find her voice to reply.

Then because she thought to hesitate might seem weak she answered:

"We are . . . engaged."

"Then let me tell you," Magnolia said, "that you are not going to marry him! And if you try to do so, you will be sorry!"

She spoke in a low voice which was venomous. Nadia could now see the fury in her eyes and it made her afraid.

"I . . . I do not understand," she answered and heard her voice stammering.

"In case you do not know, my name is Magnolia Keane, and Warren is mine, as he has always been. If he thinks he can escape me, he is very much mistaken. As for you . . ."

Magnolia looked her up and down in a way that was insulting before she finished:

". . . go back to where you came from and find another man. You shall not have mine!"

"I do not . . . know what you are . . . saying!" Nadia cried.

But Magnolia having almost spat the words at her turned away.

She walked back towards the door, moving slowly, sensuously, almost, Nadia thought, as if her body writhed like that of a snake.

Then the door was closed behind her and Nadia was alone.

For a moment she could not believe that what had happened was real.

Then she thought she could understand why Warren had been so much in love with her that when they parted he had wished to kill himself.

She could understand that with somebody like the woman she had just seen, love would not be a soft and contented happiness, but a burning, fiery rapture which would consume those who felt it.

Then when it was gone it left them sucked dry of everything but a sense of despair.

"Now I can understand," Nadia said beneath her breath. "But why, if she still wants him, does he need me?"

It all seemed incomprehensible.

She knew when Warren had told her in Paris how he had been disillusioned, she had thought he had lost the woman he loved for ever and had not expected to find her here, claiming him as obviously Magnolia Keane was doing.

She sat down on a chair because her legs felt as if they could not carry her, and tried to work it out in her own mind.

Then, because she was very intelligent, she began to understand what had happened.

Magnolia, as Warren had said, had refused to marry him because she had the chance of marrying a man with a title.

That must have been his cousin who had died through an accident.

Now the cousin was dead she wanted Warren back again, but he no longer wanted her.

It all seemed somewhat complicated.

At the same time, Nadia could understand his pride would not allow him to be thrown down and picked up again by any woman, even one as beautiful as Magnolia Keane.

"She is lovely, but dangerous!" Nadia murmured.

Then as she recalled the expression in Magnolia's eyes she felt the fear she thought she had left behind in Paris creeping over her again, the fear she had lived with for so long that it seemed cruel that it should be with her again, just when she believed she had escaped from it, and she felt herself shiver.

The door opened and Warren came in.

He looked so handsome, so elegant, in his riding-clothes with his polished boots and wearing a whip-cord jacket and there was also something strong, comforting and safe about him.

Without meaning to Nadia gave a little cry of delight.

"I was thinking of you."

Warren shut the door behind him and walked towards her.

"What was that woman doing here?" he asked. "Has she upset you?"

"How . . . how did you know she was . . . here?"

"I saw her carriage driving away," he said, "and I knew she must have called either to upset my mother, or you."

"Your mother is not yet down."

"Then you, Nadia, what did she say to you?"

Because he was still speaking sharply and his voice was hard, Nadia felt herself tremble and her face as she looked at him was very pale.

As if Warren understood, in a very different tone he said:

"You are upset, and that is the last thing

I wanted. I am very sorry, Nadia. I might
have expected this to happen."

"But . . . how could you?"

"I told her to leave my house, and she
was very angry. Then because she had
been told we were engaged, she came here
to vent her anger on you."

"She is . . . very beautiful!"

"I once thought so."

"And now?"

Nadia glanced at him and saw to her
surprise that he was smiling.

"She no longer has the power to upset
me."

"I . . . I am so very glad!"

"But she has upset you, and that is un-
forgivable!"

"No, I am all right now. It was . . . just
that she was . . . rather frightening . . . and
she said you belonged to her."

"That is where she is mistaken."

He gave a sigh as he added:

"I suppose I really should not talk to you
like this, but as you are helping me you
may as well know the truth. I was, although I would not have admitted it even
to myself, secretly afraid that when I saw
her again she would somehow get me back
into her clutches."

"And you . . . did not feel like that?"

Warren thought of how Magnolia's lips had meant nothing to him and he said:

"I am free, completely and absolutely free!"

He walked across to the window as he spoke and looked out into the sunlit garden, thinking that the beauty of it was his, just as the house, the lake, the great oaks under which the deer were lying were his.

Now he felt he could enjoy them without any shadow on his happiness.

Then behind him a soft voice said:

"P-perhaps you . . . no longer . . . need me . . . and I should . . . go away."

He turned and saw Nadia's eyes looking at him beseechingly, and knew she was afraid he might wish her to leave at once.

"Of course I want you," he said reassuringly. "Nothing could be more disastrous than for Magnolia to guess for one moment that I had brought you here just to confront her, and that as soon as she had left you had left too."

"You . . . want me to stay?"

"I insist upon your staying! That was our agreement. If you remember I said you would stay as long as I considered it necessary."

"And it is . . . really necessary? You are

not just . . . saying that to help me?"

"You are necessary to me," he said, "and I am being entirely selfish when I say I want you."

He thought the expression of relief which swept over her face was very touching and he added:

"I learnt when I was in the Army that one should never underrate the enemy, and I have the feeling, though I hope I am wrong, that Magnolia will not give up easily."

"That is what I thought . . . too," Nadia said, "but . . . surely she cannot . . . hurt you now?"

"No, of course not!" Warren replied. "The only way she could hurt me would have been through my heart, as she did before."

"And now?"

"I shall enjoy myself without giving her another thought."

"At the same time," Nadia said a little hesitatingly, "while I do not see quite what she can do, I think she might still be dangerous for you."

"Nonsense!" Warren exclaimed. "We are just frightening ourselves with 'bogey-bogeys,' as I used to do when I was a child."

Nadia laughed.

"I used to be frightened of them too."

He saw a shadow pass over her face and knew the fear had not only been when she was a child, but when she was older.

He wanted to ask her about it because he was curious, but knew it would be a mistake.

Perhaps one day she would confide in him, but for the moment he would respect her desire for secrecy.

Instead he said:

"I am going to ask you to come to luncheon to meet my relatives. Quite a lot are here already and you will meet the rest at dinner. Now, as we have plenty of time to spare, I thought perhaps you might like to drive a little way round the estate, and of course admire my house."

Nadia clasped her hands together.

"May I . . . really do that?"

"I am inviting you to come with me."

She gave a little cry of joy. Then she said:

"I will not keep you a minute while I fetch my hat."

"I am prepared to wait," he replied, "but do not be any longer than you can help."

She did not answer him, but ran from the room and he heard her footsteps crossing the hall.

He smiled and thought that although their conversation had been serious, she was still at times spontaneous and impulsive, almost child-like.

"It was clever of me to bring her here!" he murmured. "It has made it far easier to be rid of Magnolia than it would have been otherwise."

Then he wondered what his relatives would think of Nadia and was certain they would consider her far more suitable to be the Marchioness of Buckwood than Magnolia.

He was well aware that women always eyed Magnolia with suspicion, if not an active dislike.

She was far too sensational and beautiful in a way they would think somewhat immodest and theatrical.

The Marchioness of Buckwood should by tradition be beautiful, but with an indefinable dignity that came from being exceedingly well-bred, and what the servants would call 'a proper Lady.'

Strangely enough, that was exactly how Nadia looked, and Warren found himself wondering who the Charringtons were, and how she and her mother could have been left to starve.

'Charrington' was not an uncommon

name, and yet he could not remember whether he had ever met one.

"I will ask amongst my friends," he decided, "and when I go to London I will have a word with the secretary of White's."

He knew the man, who had been there for years, had every member's antecedents at his finger-tips.

Then as he realised that Nadia was running down the stairs he told himself he must be careful to remember that she was the *Comtesse* Nadia Ferrais, and she came from an old and very respected Hungarian family.

For the first time it crossed his mind that if she was Hungarian she would be expected to ride well, and for her not to do so might arouse suspicions.

He helped her into his Phaeton which drawn by two superlative horses, was waiting for them outside.

As they drove off he said:

"I have never had time to ask you before, but do you like riding?"

She looked at him and he saw her eyes were twinkling as she replied:

"I know what you are really asking me is whether I ride well enough to convince anybody who sees me that I am really an Hungarian!"

"You are reading my thoughts!"

"But of course! As you sometimes read mine!"

"Then answer my question."

"I can do that quite easily. I ride very well, but I have not ridden for a long time. Although one never forgets I shall doubtless be red and stiff after riding one of your spirited horses."

"It is something you must certainly do, once the Funeral is over."

There was a little pause. Then Nadia said:

"Perhaps you will think it was wrong of me to be so . . . extravagant, but I did insist upon *Madame* Blanc buying me a habit, just in case you asked me to ride with you."

Warren laughed, and it was a genuine sound of amusement.

"The trouble with you, Nadia, is that you are not only unpredictable, but usually one step ahead of me. It has only just occurred to me that people would expect you to ride well, while you tell me you have already anticipated that is what they would do!"

"It seemed somehow rather presumptuous when we were in Paris, but perhaps one day I shall be able to pay you back the money you have spent on me."

She made a little helpless gesture with her hands before she added:

"But for the moment . . . I cannot think how."

"You forget, it is I who am in your debt, not you in mine," Warren replied. "And I am so grateful that I want to thank you over and over again, and think of some way in which I can tell you how much your being here means to me."

He looked down at her as he spoke, and as she was looking up at him their eyes met.

It flashed through his mind that the obvious way to prove how pleased he was would be to kiss her.

For a moment it was hard to look away.

Then as if he remembered the horses needed his attention Warren looked ahead and said:

"Now you will have your first view of Buckwood, and I know you will not be disappointed."

chapter five

When the Funeral was over and the family began to leave, everybody was congratulating Warren on his engagement, and especially on Nadia.

Although he had expected them to be effusive he realised they spoke with a sincerity which had nothing to do with ordinary politeness.

He had noticed himself that after luncheon the first day and again after dinner Nadia made a point of talking to those of his relatives who were rather dull and uninteresting and would otherwise have been ignored.

He felt it was very tactful of her and could not help comparing her to Magnolia who invariably made herself the centre of attention to the male members of any party at which she appeared.

He noticed that Nadia seemed particularly kind to older women, especially those whom the other members of the family had for years, classified as bores.

When everyone had left he drove across the Park to his mother's house and found her having tea alone with Nadia in the Drawing-Room.

"We are rather late, dearest," his mother said when he came into the room, "but I felt a good cup of tea was what I needed to sustain me."

"You were marvellous, Mama!" Warren said, bending down to kiss her. "I only hope it has not been too much for you."

"It was certainly rather upsetting," his mother said quietly, "because I was very fond of Arthur. At the same time he did not linger on for months like your poor grandfather did."

Warren had always thought he would hate to die slowly with everybody thinking in the words of Charles II that he 'took an unconscionable time' in doing so.

In fact, if he had his choice he would rather die in battle or by accident, than be nothing but a body that breathed but could not think.

Because the Funeral had left him feeling sombre he tried to smile as he said:

"Now, tell me what you have planned for

this evening, although it seems incredible we should be alone. But now the family has left, it is quite eerie to have the house so quiet."

He was thinking also that it was almost unnerving to realise that it was now his, and that everybody was looking to him to bring in changes and perhaps new restrictions.

He had already made up his mind he would move slowly and try not to upset anybody.

He was well aware the old servants were set in their ways and, as Mr. Greyshott had everything running so smoothly he had no wish to ruffle on the surface what appeared to be a very calm sea.

"What I think would be best," his mother answered, "is if either you dine here with Nadia, or she comes to you. I, personally, want to retire to bed."

"You are not over-tired, Mama?" Warren asked hastily.

"No, dearest, but I hate Funerals, and also I found a great number of relatives all at the same time extremely indigestible!"

Nadia laughed, and it was a very pretty sound.

"Perhaps they would all look better if they were not draped in black," she said.

"My father always hated black. He said it was a dismal colour which only suited dismal people."

As she spoke her eyes met Warren's and they knew they were both thinking as he had told her, that *Madame* Blanc had said that women in mourning looked like black crows.

"I think as the cooks have had a lot of hard work in preparing luncheon for so many people," Warren said, "I will dine here, Mama."

"Very well, dearest, and being upstairs I shall feel that Nadia is adequately chaperoned even from the most ill-natured gossip."

"She has certainly given them enough to talk about at the moment," Warren said.

Then his eyes darkened as he remembered the same was true of Magnolia.

Unbelievably, she had come to the Funeral, even though after he had turned her out of the house he was sure that she would return to London.

Instead of which after almost everybody was seated and the Service about to begin she appeared at the West Door.

One of the ushers had hurried forward and, because Warren had not given any orders to the contrary, she was led up the aisle and squeezed into the family pew just behind where he was sitting.

She obviously intended to cause a sensation, and she was dressed in a manner which made every woman as well as every man in the congregation find it difficult to take their eyes from her.

Her gown was as elegant as the one she had been wearing the day before, but far more elaborate.

Nevertheless it revealed her figure in the same seductive manner and the long veil which fell from the small bonnet on her head and covered her face was more suitable for a widow than for an ordinary mourner.

Warren who just glanced at her was sure it was what she had worn for Raymond's Funeral and it had seemed equally sensational then.

As she knelt behind him he could smell the fragrance of her perfume, and he suspected that she was willing him to be aware of her.

All through the Service he felt as if her eyes were boring between his shoulder-blades, and although he tried to ignore her, it was impossible.

The coffin was carried down the aisle by soldiers of the County Yeomanry of which the Marquis had once been Colonel-in-Chief.

Warren walked behind it and was aware as he did so that Magnolia had pushed her way into the forefront of the other mourners.

It was then he was aware that she carried in her hand a small bouquet of white orchids.

When the coffin was lowered into the grave she dramatically threw the flowers on top of it.

Then she put her hands to her eyes, staggered, and appeared about to collapse.

Because she was standing close to him, instinctively Warren put his arms around her to prevent her from falling into the grave.

Then as he half-carried her away he was aware that while her eyes were closed there was a faint smile on her lips and she was play-acting.

He handed her over to another member of the family as quickly as he could.

At the same time he was furiously angry that she had indulged in a sensational scene which would lose nothing in the telling.

There would also, he was quite sure, be reports in the local newspapers.

After such outrageous behaviour he was not surprised when the whole party arrived back at the house to find Magnolia ensconced in a comfortable chair in the Drawing-Room with one of the maids ministering to her with smelling-salts.

He made no effort to speak to her, but other members of the family went to her side, and Warren could hear her lamenting in a low but clear voice how much she would miss the Marquis.

"He was always so kind to me," he heard her say, "and I shall not only miss him but this house. I feel as if it is my home, and I cannot bear to lose it!"

There was a most convincing little sob in her voice as she said the last words.

Warren thought, although it might have been his imagination, that one or two of the relatives glanced at him as if they thought he had the answer to her problem.

It was not until she left almost immediately after luncheon, so as to receive the maximum amount of attention, with half of the men present going to the front door to see her off, that Warren was able to heave a sigh of relief.

"Now there is no excuse for her to come back again," he told himself, although he had the uncomfortable feeling that she might try.

He wished then that he had asked Nadia to attend the Funeral luncheon and made it clear then that the date of their marriage would be announced as soon as possible.

Yet since she had met all the family the previous day he had thought it unnecessary for her to appear to be mourning the Marquis whom she had never met.

As soon as Magnolia had gone he therefore made a point of saying to all his relatives as he bade them goodbye:

"I hope when you come here again it will be in much happier circumstances."

It was impossible for them not to realise what he meant, and the majority of them replied automatically:

"You mean your wedding, Warren dear!"

"I think perhaps we should have an engagement party before that," he said with a smile. "It could not of course be a Ball, but perhaps a garden-party or a Reception at the beginning of August."

"We will look forward to it!" everybody exclaimed.

He knew that for the family any party at Buckwood was always hailed as something particularly enjoyable.

Now looking at Nadia across the tea-table he thought how attractive she looked in a gown that appeared simple, but had all the elegance that only France could create for a woman.

Even though she was still very thin, there was colour in her cheeks that had not been there before, and while her eyes were still too large for her face there was a light in them that seemed as if she had captured the sunlight.

"Tomorrow," he said, "I suggest as I have the farms to visit and it would be far quicker to ride than to drive, that you accompany me on horse-back."

There was no need for Nadia to speak in order to express her excitement, since the look on her face did it for her.

Then Warren's mother said:

"I know how thrilled and delighted everybody will be to meet Nadia, but if you go to one farm you must visit them all, otherwise there will be a great deal of jealousy."

"I have already thought of that," Warren replied. "I remember how in the old days when I called at the farms they always said:

" 'We've not seen ye're mother lately! Tell her I've a pot of home-made jam waiting for her.' "

His mother laughed.

"Or else it was a jar of pickles or honey, or a cut of the newly-cured ham. The people here have always been so generous!"

She put out her hand to touch Nadia on the arm.

"I know they will love you, my dear," she said. "I noticed today how kind you were to the older members of the family."

Nadia laughed.

"Mama always said if at a party there was somebody left out or alone, it showed that one was a bad hostess."

"That is true! At the same time, most young people are too busy thinking about themselves to have time for those who are no longer young."

The way his mother spoke told Warren very clearly how much she approved of Nadia, and he congratulated himself for being so lucky as to have found somebody who would play the part so well.

He had never realised until his mother told him so that she had not liked Magnolia nor had she thought her good enough for him. So it was slightly surprising that she had taken so quickly to Nadia.

He was just holding out his cup for his mother to refill it when a footman came into the room with a package on a silver salver.

"What is it, James?" Lady John asked.

"This 'as been left for th' Countess, M'Lady."

As he spoke he held out the salver towards Nadia who looked at it in surprise.

"For me?" she asked.

"I cannot believe it is a wedding-present already," Warren joked.

Nadia took the parcel from the salver which seemed to be a small box.

She looked at it, thinking there must be some mistake, saw it was addressed in capital letters very clearly: "THE COUNTESS NADIA FERRAIS."

"Open it!" Warren said. "It must be a present, although it seems surprising that any of my relatives should be so generous so quickly."

"Now, darling, that is rather unkind!" his mother reproached him. "Ever since you were small the family always spoilt you with gifts at Christmas and on your birthday, and you used to complain bitterly when I made you write and thank for them."

"That is true," Warren said, "and you taught me never to 'look a gift-horse in the mouth!' "

His mother laughed, and by this time Nadia had undone the outer covering of the parcel to find a box of chocolates.

They came from Gunters in Berkeley Square who were famous for their special sweet-meats which Warren had often bought for his mother.

She had now however a touch of diabetes and her doctor had forbidden her to eat anything containing sugar.

Nadia looked first at the box, then at the paper in which it had been wrapped before she said:

"It does not say who sent it."

"I expect the servant who took it at the door will know," Warren replied.

Nadia undid the ribbon that tied the box, opened it and said:

"They certainly look very delicious! Will you have one?"

"Not now," Warren replied. "Perhaps after dinner."

"I am not allowed chocolates," Lady John said, "so you will have to eat them all yourself, my dear."

"Not after such a big tea!" Nadia protested.

She looked at Warren as she spoke, and he knew she was telling him she was making a tremendous effort to eat, but was still finding it difficult.

She was just about to put the lid back on the box when Lady John said:

"Look at greedy Bertha!"

Ever since Warren had come home the two dogs which had always been at his uncle's side had attached themselves to him.

One was a fairly young spaniel who he knew was an exceptionally good gun-dog, the other a bitch who had been a field-trial winner in her day, but was now very old, crippled with rheumatism and finding it hard to see.

But ever since his arrival she had been at his heels and now had followed him into the house where she had lain down quietly beside his chair.

Now however Bertha was sitting up on her hind legs begging.

Nadia looked at her in surprise and Lady John explained:

"Poor Arthur developed a very sweet tooth in his old age and one of the reasons why he grew so fat, which undoubtedly contributed to his heart-attack, was that he was always eating chocolates."

She looked at Bertha and smiled as she added:

"Bertha is as greedy about them as he was. As you can see, her mouth is watering as she can sense what you have in your hands."

"Then she must certainly be the first to

156

enjoy my present," Nadia said.

She picked out what she thought was a soft-centred chocolate and held it out to Bertha who quickly gobbled it up, then was sitting up begging for more.

"That is enough," Warren said. "She will get so fat that she will be slower than she is already."

"Just one more," Nadia pleaded.

She smiled at him as she spoke, and held out another chocolate to Bertha.

The dog snatched it from her, then suddenly as she did so, she seemed to shake all over.

So quickly that the three people watching could hardly believe it was happening, she turned and rolled over on her back.

For a few seconds every muscle in her body seemed to be twitching.

Then suddenly she was completely still.

Nadia gave a little cry and asked:

"What has happened? Has she had a fit?"

Warren went down on his knees beside Bertha.

He was feeling for her heart. Then he said: "She is dead!"

"It cannot be true!" Lady John exclaimed. "How should it happen so suddenly?"

"Because she was poisoned!" Warren replied.

157

He reached out and took the box of chocolates from Nadia's lap, then he put his arms around his mother and lifted her to her feet.

"I want you to come upstairs and rest, Mama," he said. "I am going to send for the Veterinary Surgeon to examine both Bertha and the chocolates. Something unpleasant is happening, and I do not want it to upset you."

"But it does upset me!" his mother protested. "How could anybody be so wicked, so evil, as to give poisoned chocolates to Nadia?"

Warren knew the answer, but he did not reply.

Instead he led his mother across the room and Nadia followed them.

She was very pale and her heart was beating frantically with a fear which had been her constant companion for nearly three years.

Now she told herself that there was no escape from it, not even in England.

She did not see Warren again until dinner-time.

When Lady John had gone to rest, Nadia had gone to her own room, having been urged to rest also.

Instead she could only lie in the comfortable bed, watching through the open window the sun sinking behind the trees, and hearing the rooks making their usual noise as they went to roost.

"How can this have happened?" she kept asking.

She knew if Bertha's death had not warned them, she undoubtedly would have died, and perhaps Warren as well if, as he had said he would, he had eaten one of the chocolates after dinner.

The whole idea was so terrifying that even though it was very hot outside she felt herself shivering beneath the sheet that covered her.

It was so unexpected after she had begun to feel relaxed and happy for the first time, with somebody as kind and sweet as Lady John, who reminded her of her mother.

Warren had also given her a wonderful feeling of security every moment she was with him.

Poisoned chocolates! How could it be possible? How could anybody think of doing anything so diabolical, except those who had haunted her thoughts and dreams for so long?

Because she was so frightened, Nadia prayed:

"Please, God, do not let me die like that!

Please let me live a little longer."

Then as she felt her prayer winging up into the sky, she thought it strange how only a few days ago she had longed to die, and now she wanted to live.

She knew it was because Warren had saved her.

He had brought her away from a world in which everything was ugly, sordid and painful to a place where everything was beautiful and until this moment she had thought peaceful and normal.

Now she was aware that it was very different and she felt an irrepressible fear.

She might so easily have put one of the chocolates in her own mouth, just because she thought it would please Warren that she was eating.

The colour had left her face and her eyes were dark and troubled when after her maid had helped her dress she had gone downstairs to dinner.

She had wanted to say goodnight to Lady John, but her lady's-maid had told her she was already half-asleep, and it would be a mistake to disturb her.

"Supposing she had died?" Nadia asked herself. "It would have been my fault, and I would have felt I was a murderess!"

She was early, so she had not expected

the Marquis had yet arrived, but when she went into the Drawing-Room, he was standing at one of the open windows, a glass of champagne in his hand.

He turned towards her and watched her walk into the room, aware without her having to say one word, what she was feeling.

He gave her the glass he was holding, then returned to the side-table to pour another glass of champagne from the bottle that was standing in an ice-cooler.

When he came back to her side in a voice he could hardly hear she asked:

"What . . . did you . . . find out?"

"What I suspected," he answered, "that the chocolates had had a poison injected into them very skilfully! It would have been impossible for you to realise they had been tampered with until it was too late!"

He saw the shudder that shook Nadia's body. Then she said:

"I must go away. I . . . cannot stay here . . . because they must have . . . found me, and if they . . . strike again, it might . . . harm you!"

She was speaking without thinking. Then she saw the expression of astonishment in Warren's eyes before he asked:

"What are you talking about?"

161

She looked at him blindly for a moment, then away again, and he said quietly:

"I think we should be honest about this, and face facts. The poisoned chocolates came from Magnolia Keane!"

He realised as he spoke that this was not what Nadia had been thinking.

She stared at him for a long moment before she asked a little incoherently:

"Are you . . . sure of that? Are you . . . quite sure?"

"Absolutely sure, and the only question the Surgeon kept asking me was how anybody who was not experienced could have inserted poison so skilfully without there being any outward sign of it."

Nadia drew in her breath.

Then in a voice Warren was aware she was trying to make normal she asked:

"But . . . why should Miss . . . Keane wish to . . . poison me?"

Warren's voice was hard as he replied:

"I should have thought that was obvious."

"Yes . . . of course . . . how stupid of me!" Nadia said. "She did say that . . . you belonged to her . . . and she would never let me . . . have you."

"Tell me exactly what she said."

It was an order and although Nadia hesitated she knew she must obey him.

"She said first: 'I understand you are trying to marry Warren!' "

"And what did you reply?"

"I said we were engaged."

"Then what happened?"

Again Warren's voice was very authoritative and Nadia replied:

"Miss Keane said: 'You are not going to marry him, and if you try to do so, you will be sorry!' "

As she spoke Nadia thought it was very stupid of her not to have thought in the first place that it might be Magnolia Keane who had sent her the chocolates.

She had never imagined any English Lady would behave in such a manner, or that it was possible for her to be in that sort of danger in an English country house where there were servants to protect them and Warren never very far away.

"I can only say how sorry I am, and it is my fault that she has upset you," Warren said in a quiet voice. "I thought she might, in some way I could not even imagine, try to hurt me, but it never struck me that she would attempt to murder you!"

"Perhaps it would be . . . better if you m-married her as she . . . wants you to do," Nadia said almost in a whisper. "After all . . . you . . . loved her once."

Even as she spoke, as she had done spontaneously on a sudden impulse, she knew that she could not bear Warren to marry such a woman.

He was too fine, too noble, far too magnificent to waste himself on anyone who would stoop to murder to get her own way.

Then she saw the scowl between Warren's eyes and realised how angry he was as he said:

"I would not even try to save Magnolia from the gallows, which is where she would have ended had it not been for poor Bertha."

"The Veterinary Surgeon could not . . . save her?"

"She died instantly, as you would have done if you had eaten the chocolates as Magnolia intended you should."

His lips tightened before he said:

"She had not foreseen that I would be here, but would still be looking after some of the relatives who might be expected to linger until it was quite late."

His voice was deep with anger as he continued:

"She knew that Mama was not allowed chocolates, and that left only you, who she expected would be here alone when you received her present."

As hc finished, he gave an exclamation which seemed almost like an oath as he added:

"That is what happened, and there is nothing I can do about it, no charge I can bring against her, although only by a miracle are you alive!"

Without thinking Nadia moved and held onto him with both her hands.

"It is frightening . . . very frightening," she said, "but at least you did not eat one . . . as you might have done after dinner."

"Bertha saved us, and we should be grateful for that," Warren said. "I have left orders for her to be buried in the Dogs' Cemetery where all our dogs lie, and where I like to believe they are happy and undisturbed."

For the first time since she had come into the room, Nadia smiled.

"We, too, had a Cemetery for our dogs," she said. "When I was a little girl I used to put a bone on their graves thinking they could eat it when nobody was there, and it had always disappeared in the morning!"

"Where was your Cemetery?" Warren asked.

As if Nadia realised she had been indiscreet she took her hands from his and said quickly:

"We were talking about poor Bertha, and tomorrow I would like to see where she is buried."

"You were also telling me about your dogs," Warren said. "What sort were they?"

"I do not . . . want to . . . talk about it," Nadia replied. "You must tell me how I can be . . . safe from Miss Keane . . . and perhaps for your sake . . . I should . . . go away."

She knew as she spoke she had no wish to leave him. In fact, it would be very frightening to have to do so.

As if he knew what she was feeling Warren reached out and took her hand in both of his.

"Now listen to me, Nadia," he said, "I promise I will look after and protect you, and that I shall prevent anything like this ever happening again."

He felt her fingers quiver in his and after a moment he asked:

"You still trust me?"

"You know I do," Nadia said.

Then as she looked up into his eyes it was impossible for either of them to look away.

After a dinner at which Nadia had tried

to eat a little of each course, they went back into the Drawing-Room.

The last dying rays of the sun were crimson on the horizon, and as they instinctively walked towards the open window the peace and fragrance of the garden made it impossible to believe there was danger and hatred in the world beyond it.

They walked towards the sun-dial and stood looking down at the ancient figures carved in the worn stone.

"I want you to be happy here," Warren said, as if he was pursuing his own thoughts.

"I am happy," Nadia answered, "and now I am no longer afraid of Miss Keane . . . or anything . . . else."

He knew from the way she spoke the last few words that she was in some other kind of danger, which she kept a secret, that was very different from what had just occurred.

Warren longed to ask her once again to tell him the truth about herself, but he knew it would only upset her, and he was certain that she would refuse, as she had already, to satisfy his curiosity.

She looked so lovely, and at the same time so fragile and insubstantial in the fading light, that he thought it seemed almost absurd that she should be involved in such dramatic and dangerous circumstances.

"I have not had a chance to tell you," he said, "how magnificently you played your part yesterday. All my relatives were captivated by you, and think I am very lucky to have found such a suitable wife to reign at Buckwood."

"'They were all very kind to me," Nadia said in a low voice, "and your mother has been . . . wonderful!"

"My mother says you are everything she hoped for in a daughter-in-law."

"I am sure she is very upset by what has just occurred."

"After I saw the Veterinary Surgeon I explained to her who was responsible, and she merely said it did not surprise her."

"But she feels afraid . . . as I am . . . that Miss Keane might try to . . . hurt you."

"I do not think she wants to kill *me*," Warren remarked.

Nadia gave a little cry and once again put up her hands towards him.

"If she cannot get her way . . . if you do not marry her after all . . . even after she had . . . disposed of me . . . then she will . . . hate you for not doing what she wishes . . . and might try to avenge herself . . . as you are doing."

168

The last words were very faint, but Warren heard them.

Then as if he thought it was a mistake to be too serious, he said lightly:

"I am quite certain that whatever happens you will save me, as you have done already, very effectively."

"Have I . . . really been able to help you?"

"You know you have," he answered. "If you had not been here, Magnolia somehow in some crafty way of her own might have persuaded my relatives that I was under an obligation to make her my wife. That was what I foresaw and feared when I asked for your help."

There was silence. Then Nadia said hesitatingly:

"I . . . I thought perhaps now you would . . . want me to . . . go away . . . but I can see that might be a mistake."

"A very great mistake," Warren agreed. "I want you to stay here, I want you to go on playing the part of my *fiancée* until we are both absolutely convinced that Magnolia will try no more tricks."

After a moment he added:

"Perhaps I am asking too much of you? You have been through so much already in your own life, although you will not tell me about it, and I should not ask you to risk being murdered by a jealous woman who is obviously mentally unhinged."

Nadia smiled at him, and he thought it was a very brave and rather touching little smile.

"You promised to protect me."

"And that is what I will do," he answered, "but, please, Nadia, stay. I want to have you help me getting to know the people who are now mine, and when it comes to planning alterations or improvements, two brains are obviously better than one."

"I think you are flattering me," Nadia replied, "and really you are quite capable of doing all those things without any help at all! At the same time, you know I want to stay here."

He knew there was a fear behind the words that she would not express or explain, and he said with the smile that many women had found irresistible:

"I am pleading with you to stay! In fact, I should be very hurt and upset if you run away and leave me."

"Then I will not do so."

"Now I am going to send you to bed," Warren said. "When I said goodnight to Mama she said that if she needed her beauty-sleep, so did you, and as you are aware, I want you to look very much fatter than you are at the moment."

Nadia laughed and the sound seemed to ring out like music in the quietness of the garden.

"I keep forgetting now that I have such lovely gowns that you are shocked by my appearance," she said. "I really am trying very, very hard to eat, but you will have to give me time."

"I can think of quite a lot of things I should give you as well as time," Warren answered, "but you will have to wait until I get to London."

He had forgotten as he spoke that Nadia was unlike every other woman he had ever met, wanting everything he was ready to give her, and pleading for a great deal more besides.

Nadia took her hand from his and said in a serious little voice which he knew so well:

"Please . . . I have accepted these beautiful gowns from you because I could hardly appear as your *fiancée* in the threadbare dress which was all I possessed. But I do not expect . . . anything else, and I should be very . . . upset if you tried to give it to me."

Warren thought for a moment. Then he said:

"Surely you must be aware that everybody will expect me to give you, as my *fiancée* all the things that would express my love rather more eloquently than words."

"No!" Nadia said.

She spoke so firmly that Warren was surprised.

Then as if she felt she must explain herself she said:

"When you asked me to help you, you said you thought of me as a lady. So as a lady, I will not and cannot accept anything from you except what is absolutely essential for the part I have to play."

She spoke with a dignity that was very impressive.

Then she added in a child-like and very pleading voice:

"I know Mama would not have approved . . . so please . . . do not embarrass me."

Warren knew there was nothing he could do but capitulate and he said:

"Very well, Nadia, but I can only say that you are a very unusual and very surprising young woman, and apart from that, somebody I respect and admire for the courage you have shown."

Because of the way he spoke he saw the

colour flood into Nadia's cheeks.

Then as her eye-lids flickered and he knew that she was too shy to look at him, he thought it was very attractive, very endearing, and in every way very different from Magnolia.

chapter six

Nadia walked round the sitting room looking at the pictures and ornaments.

Every time she did so she thought how beautiful they were and how each one had a history of its own which she wanted to remember.

She had asked Warren about the pictures and he told her how they had come into the family, one of them being a present to his father and mother on their marriage.

"Everything in this house Mama treasures because it is part of her life with my father, and of course mine," he said with a smile.

"I knew it was all chosen with love," Nadia said softly.

He smiled, thinking it was the sort of remark that only she could make, and which he found himself remembering when he thought about her during the night.

For her, he felt sure, every day was an enchantment which she could not express in words.

He knew that her sufferings, which must remain a secret, were something she did not wish to talk about because they had been so painful and had resulted in her mother's death.

But he could not be unaware that for Nadia to have come to Buckwood was like being lifted from the horrors and terrors of hell into a special Heaven which was filled with sunshine.

"How could I have wanted to die, when I can live here?" Nadia asked herself.

Then as always, when she reflected how marvellous everything was, there was a little stab of pain in case it should suddenly all come to an end.

She would wake in the night, thinking how wonderful the previous day had been and how much she was looking forward to the next.

Then she would ask herself how many days there could be before Warren told her that her usefulness was at an end.

It was such an agony to think of it that she tried to force herself to live for the day, the hour, the second, and miss nothing.

Now as she looked at the Sir Joshua

Reynolds portrait over the mantelpiece she knew she was thinking it was something she would never forget, and wherever she might be she would see it in her mind's eye.

The same applied to the 'Conversation Piece' which was particularly important because it portrayed Warren's ancestor and his family with Buckwood House in the background.

'He has everything,' she thought.

Then she was ashamed of feeling a touch of envy being herself homeless.

"I wish I could be in a picture and live there like the people the artist has portrayed, then I would be immortal!"

It was a fantasy which she found intriguing, and she imagined herself, if not in that particular picture, then being painted by some famous artist who would portray her body while she would give it her heart and soul.

She played with the idea because it delighted her and tried to think what would be a suitable background.

"As I do not own a house," she told herself, "it would be more appropriate if I were out in a garden."

Thinking of it made her walk through the window towards the sun-dial, and standing by it as she had done with Warren she touched the figures engraved on top of it.

Then she heard a strange sound which came from a door in the red brick wall.

Nadia knew it led out into an orchard where the apples on the trees were just beginning to change colour.

She wondered what the sound could be, and going down the flagstoned path which was bordered on each side of a well-trimmed box hedge she pulled upon the ancient door which had been there as long as the walls themselves.

When she could not hear anything she moved a few steps into the orchard still wondering what the sound had been.

The next moment she gave a cry of sheer terror for something heavy and dark was thrown over her head.

Before she could even struggle she was picked up and carried swiftly away, in what direction she had no idea.

Warren was in his Study dealing with a pile of correspondence which Mr. Greyshott had left for him to sign.

There were several new leases for tenants who had taken over farms that had remained empty during his uncle's illness, and there was also a report from the Manager of his estate in Devonshire which had to be read carefully.

He thought as he did so that he would soon have to visit his other properties, and especially the one at Newmarket where his uncle had kept most of his racehorses.

In the meantime however there was still a great deal to do here.

He had already had a number of calls from prominent people in the County inviting him to take up various positions of importance which it would have been impossible for him to refuse.

He was just reading a letter from the Deputy Lord Lieutenant who had taken over his uncle's duties while he was ill, when Mr. Greyshott came into the room.

He looked up and Mr. Greyshott said:

"I thought you would like to know, My Lord, that I have just seen the Veterinary Surgeon who confirms that the poison which was inserted into the chocolates was, as I suspected, taken from here!"

Warren frowned.

He had been very angry when Mr. Greyshott had told him that he guessed that the poison which might have killed Nadia had actually come from the house.

Apparently his uncle had an aversion to

shooting any of his horses or dogs that had become too old or too ill to go on living, and had trusted nobody but himself to 'put them to sleep.'

He had therefore persuaded the Veterinary Surgeon to find him a poison that was so strong and acted so quickly that the animal died almost immediately it was swallowed.

What had first puzzled Warren was to know where Magnolia could have so quickly obtained a deadly poison which had killed Bertha.

It was then that Mr. Greyshott, who was the only person to be let into the secret of the poisoned chocolates, said that he recognised the box from Gunter's which had been ordered by the Marquis before he was taken ill.

Secondly, he suspected the poison itself came from a locked cupboard in the Gun-Room where the Marquis had kept it, thinking it would be impossible for anybody to get hold of it without his permission.

"Why should Miss Keane have known of it?" Warren enquired.

"I imagine your cousin told her," Mr. Greyshott replied, "or perhaps His Lordship did so. They both often spoke of how distressing it was to dispose of any of the animals they loved."

He thought for a moment before he added:

"I remember now that while Miss Keane was staying here the Marquis put one of his dogs who was suffering severely from a growth in the throat, out of its misery."

"So I suppose," Warren said, "Miss Keane took the poison with her when I turned her out of the house."

Mr. Greyshott paused for a moment before he answered:

"Actually, the cupboard had been broken into and the lock smashed!"

There was nothing more to say. At the same time Warren had insisted on an autopsy which Mr. Greyshott now handed to him.

Because it only confirmed what he already knew, he set it to one side and started to talk of matters concerning the estate until Mr. Greyshott left him so that he could finish signing his letters.

"I will come back for them in half-an-hour, My Lord."

Some of the letters were quite long, and Warren had only completed half-a-dozen when the door opened again and without raising his head he remarked:

"You are too quick for me, Greyshott. I have not yet finished!"

There was no answer and he looked up, then stiffened.

It was Magnolia who had come into the Study looking exceedingly alluring, and no longer in mourning.

She was wearing a very elaborate gown of rose pink chiffon inset with lace that made her look more exotic than usual, and her wide-brimmed hat was trimmed with flowers and ribbons of the same colour.

For a moment Warren just stared at her. Then he rose slowly to his feet, as if he was resentful at having to do so.

Magnolia walked slowly, as if deliberately displaying herself before him, towards the desk.

Only as she reached it did Warren ask:

"What are you doing here, Magnolia? You know I have no wish to see you."

"But I have every wish to see you, dearest Warren," Magnolia replied, "and I think when you hear what I have to say, you will realise it would be wise to listen to me."

"I do not want to listen, and we have nothing to say to each other," Warren said firmly. "Go away, Magnolia, and leave me alone!"

He sat down again as he spoke and looked at her, across the desk wondering whether he should accuse her of trying to murder Nadia or whether it would be better to say nothing.

She was looking at him seductively, and he thought her eyes which seemed half-veiled by her long lashes had a glint of triumph in them he did not understand.

She was holding a paper in her hand, which she put down on the edge of the desk and there was something seductive about the way she slowly drew off her long kid-gloves.

Then she put out her left hand and asked:

"Do you see what I am wearing?"

Because he was puzzled by her behaviour Warren looked down and saw on the third finger of her left hand she was wearing a ring he had given her.

He could so well remember purchasing it in Bond Street, then giving it to her and kissing first the ring, then her finger before he said:

"Because it is impossible at the moment, my darling, for us to become engaged or married, I am binding you to me with a ring that symbolises that you are mine for eternity."

"Oh, dearest, that is what I want," Magnolia had exclaimed.

"And you will never escape me!" Warren replied. "Although you cannot wear this ring in the daytime until we can announce our engagement, I want you to promise me you will wear it at night when you dream of me."

"You know I will do that."

She had looked down at the ring which was a very pretty one with small diamonds set with gold all round it.

She had then lifted her lips and Warren had kissed her passionately, possessively, until they were both breathless.

Now the memory of what he had felt at that moment made Warren feel disgusted and he said harshly:

"I told you to go away! If you do not do so, I shall ring for the servants to show you out."

"I doubt if you will do that after you have heard what I have to say," Magnolia replied.

Now she picked up the paper she had put on the edge of the desk and said with a note in her voice he did not understand:

"I have here a Marriage Licence made out in your name and mine!"

"What the devil are you talking about?" Warren exclaimed.

"It will be easy for us to be married immediately," Magnolia said. "I have made enquiries and the Vicar is at this moment at home in his Vicarage."

"I can only imagine you are insane!" he replied. "I would no more marry you than I would marry the Devil himself!"

He spoke violently because his temper was rising, but Magnolia remained quite unmoved.

She merely set the Special Licence down in front of him before she said:

"If you do not marry me, then that woman you call your *fiancée* will die!"

Warren seemed for the moment to be turned to stone before he enquired in a voice which with a deliberate effort he made quiet and calm:

"I should be interested to know exactly what you mean by that!"

"I mean," Magnolia replied, "that she has been taken to a place where you will never find her and where, if you do not marry me as I have asked you to do, she will die of starvation!"

For a moment there was silence.

"I do not believe you!" Warren exclaimed.

Magnolia looked at him under her eyelashes and smiled, making the whole conversation seem more horrifying than ever.

He knew she was deliberately being seductive, being quite confident that it would be impossible for him not to respond.

Then she lifted her face to his in a manner that was contrived because she knew it displayed the curves of her long, swan-like neck.

"The young woman has been carried away from the garden at your mother's house and hidden so that clever though you are, my dearest Warren, you will never be able to find her."

She shrugged her shoulders so that it displayed the sinuous lissomness of her figure before she added:

"Even if you search and eventually find her, it will be too late, for she will, as I have said, die of starvation."

Warren drew in his breath as if he still could not credit what he was hearing.

He looked down then at the Special Licence lying in front of him and saw on it was written his own name and that of Magnolia.

He knew her well enough to realise that she was wildly elated by the feeling that she had him cornered, and that there was, she believed, nothing he could do but accept her terms or else allow Nadia to die.

After a moment he said quietly:

"Surely we can come to some better solution than that I should accept what, as you well know, Magnolia, is criminal blackmail?"

Magnolia gave a little laugh.

"Fine words! And they mean there is nothing you can do, my adored one, but make me your wife!"

Warren wanted to shout at her that nothing and nobody would make him do that.

Then in his mind's eye he saw again Nadia's face as he had seen it when he saved her from drowning herself in the Seine, and had realised she was suffering from starvation.

He had been well aware how in the last five days since they had been at Buckwood the marks of privation were gradually disappearing day by day and almost hour by hour.

It had given her a new beauty.

He had seen as her chin became less sharp, the bones in her wrists less prominent, and the lines at the sides of her mouth and under her eyes disappeared, she looked as young as her years.

And when she was animated and laughing she was so beautiful that he thought it was difficult to recognise the unhappy, frightened girl who had wanted to die.

He was sensible enough however, to know that if she was subjected again to such privation it might be difficult to save her a second time.

Almost as if she was following his thoughts Magnolia said with what was now an undoubted note of triumph in her voice:

"It is no use, Warren! Clever and brilliant though you may be, I have won this time!"

She paused and when he did not speak she added:

"And, darling, when we are married I will make it up to you. I shall be everything you want in a wife and very much more as a woman that you love."

She gave a little laugh before she added:

"I know that nobody could be a more ardent and more passionate lover than you, and however much my brain wanted to marry a coronet, my body has always responded to yours, and now we will be very happy."

As she finished speaking she realised that

Warren was not listening. He merely asked, and his voice was sharp:

"Tell me where you have put Nadia!"

"Of course I will do that, just as soon as we are married. We can go now to the Church and you can tell your carriage to follow us. As soon as you replace this ring on my finger, we will send him to find that woman, but keep her out of my sight!"

Magnolia spoke sharply and it told Warren how much she hated Nadia because she thought she had taken her place. He was certain there would be no chance of saving her unless he did as she demanded.

Once again he stared down at the Special Licence on his desk, trying frantically to think what he could do.

It flashed through his mind that he could ring the bell and call for the servants.

A search could be made, organised by Mr. Greyshott, all over the estate.

It would cause a great deal of gossip and scandal and might eventually reach the newspapers.

He knew nothing could be more damaging from his own point of view, or that of his family.

He also had the uncomfortable knowledge that it would be appallingly difficult to find Nadia without having the slightest clue as to where Magnolia had hidden her.

He owned around Buckwood five thousand acres of land, and all the time he had been away in Africa, Magnolia had been staying here with Raymond except when they were together in London.

She would by now know hundreds of places where somebody small and weak like Nadia could lie for weeks, even months before she could be found.

In addition to his blotter, on which the Buckwood coat-of-arms was embossed in gold, were all the items that were considered essential to a gentleman's desk.

There was a large gold ink-pot, a pen-tray, a pot containing game-shot in which pens could be cleaned, a tiny candle in a very elegant candlestick which was used to heat the sealing-wax with which he sealed his letters.

There was also a gold ruler, a pair of gold scissors, and a gold letter-opener, all bearing the Buckwood crest.

As if another part of his brain had taken over, Warren noticed that the letter-opener was long and very sharp, and suddenly he knew what he must do.

"Give me your hand," he said aloud and held out his towards Magnolia.

She did not seem surprised, but put her hand in his on which was the ring he had given her and as his fingers closed over it she smiled into his eyes seductively.

It was then that with the letter-opener Warren slashed her sharply across the back of the hand.

Magnolia started, then gave a shrill scream.

As she did so she looked incredulously at the long wound from which the blood was already oozing.

She would have snatched her hand away but Warren held tightly onto it as he rose to his feet.

Still holding onto her he walked around the desk until they were facing each other.

"How dare you cut me!" Magnolia screamed at him. "You have hurt me, Warren, you have hurt me terribly!"

"I am going to hurt you a great deal more," he said, in a quiet voice, "unless you tell me where you have hidden Nadia."

"My hand is bleeding!"

Warren glanced down and saw the blood was actually running over the side of her hand onto his own.

Still in the same quiet manner in which he had spoken before he said:

"It will undoubtedly leave a nasty scar

and if you do not tell me immediately what I wish to know, I will scar your face in the same way, first on one side, then on the other."

"You would not dare!"

The words were defiant but he could see as she recoiled away from him the fear in her eyes.

"You have driven me far enough," Warren said, "and I shall not hesitate to disfigure you. Now which shall it be?"

He raised the letter-opener as he spoke and now Magnolia could see its long, sharp end almost like a stiletto pointing towards her.

For a moment it seemed as if she would go on fighting him.

Then as if she knew she was defeated she surrendered.

"Very well," she said sullenly, "she is in the Slate-Mine."

"You are not lying to me?"

"No!"

"If you have deceived me," Warren warned, "I swear I will find you and carry out my threat!"

He paused before he added:

"Make no mistake, Magnolia! I shall mark you and make certain that in the future your beauty shall not blind another fool to the vileness of your character!"

As he spoke Warren took his hand from Magnolia's so suddenly that because she was straining away from him she almost fell to the ground.

Then as she staggered to keep her balance he flung the letter-opener down on the floor, and walking out of the room slammed the door behind him.

The men who had carried Nadia away from the garden had put her in a carriage which set off quickly the moment they closed the door.

They had thrown her down roughly on the seat and she was aware they had got into the carriage after her and were sitting opposite with their backs to the horses.

She was so frightened that for a moment she could not think and was finding it hard to breathe because of the thickness of the cloth which covered her.

She could feel her whole body trembling and her lips were dry.

Although she wanted to scream it was impossible to do so, and anyway she was quite certain nobody would hear her crying for help.

She was also frightened that the men might strike her to keep her quiet.

Then, because she thought they were the same men who had pursued her and her mother across Europe, she prayed she might die.

She knew it would be impossible to face what might lie in store for her and remain sane.

"Let me die, please God, let me die!" she whispered in her heart, and at the same time she prayed for Warren.

"Save me! Save me!" she cried out to him.

Then she knew he could not help her and somehow she must find a way to kill herself before the men sitting on the other side of the carriage killed her in an agonising way.

She was so frightened that she could feel her teeth chattering and the tears running down her cheeks.

Then she heard one of the men speak to the other.

"Be it far?" he asked.

"Nay," the other man replied. "We be nearly there."

It was then Nadia felt a relief that was so overwhelming that she felt almost as if she was free instead of a captive!

No one could mistake the voices of the men in the carriage for anything but English, and she had feared something very different.

Her captors, she then knew, had been ordered to abduct her by Magnolia Keane.

It was frightening, but not as terrifying as she had thought it a few moments ago when she had known she must die.

Then, because she was sure it was Magnolia Keane who had sent these men to kidnap her, somehow, although she could not think how, she knew that Warren would save her.

She was certain, so certain that once again she was praying to him to come to her rescue, feeling as if she sent her thoughts towards him on wings.

'Save me! Save me!'

She could almost see him listening to her plea for help, his grey eyes reassuring her.

It was then, at that moment, almost as if it was a blinding light in the suffocating darkness, that she knew she loved him.

She loved him and she had done so for a long time, but had not realised it was love.

She had known it was a joy beyond words to ride with him, to talk with him, and that every time he came into the room she felt as if her heart leapt towards him because he looked so strong and so handsome.

"I love him!" she told herself. "I love him, but I am nothing to him, except as somebody he has hired to help him get rid of that wicked, murderous woman!"

Almost without thinking, her prayer to Warren became one of gratitude to God because he had not married Magnolia Keane, nor did he want her any more as his wife.

How could he, when she had attempted murder, and had only failed in what she had set out to do because a dog was greedy?

Nadia had lain all that night feeling the horror of what had occurred was like something cold and hard pressing into her breast.

It was only after she had been alone with Warren the next day, visiting the farms as he had asked her to do, that the pain had gone away, and when she was with him she could forget about it.

Now she knew that Magnolia was trying once again to murder her, and the only person who could save her from death was Warren.

"Save me! Save me!" she cried out in her breast.

Yet she was afraid the men would shoot or stab her before Warren could reach her.

Then because she was very intelligent, Nadia worked out in her mind that if they were going to kill her they might have done so without taking her away from the garden.

If they had intended to drown her, the lake was quite handy, but now they were driving away from it, although in which direction Nadia was not sure.

Their only alternative, she thought, was to throw her into a deep pit, or imprison her somewhere so that she could not escape and would therefore eventually die slowly and miserably of starvation.

It was all very frightening, except for a faint ray of hope still lingering that Warren would defeat Magnolia's nefarious plan, even at the last moment.

It was almost, Nadia thought, as if it was a battle between the two of them, a battle of love which had turned to one of hatred.

They were therefore all the more vindictive, more violent, because they had once felt so differently towards each other.

She reasoned it all out and somehow, although she was still terrified, she felt as if God was on her side and good must triumph over evil.

The carriage came to a halt and she heard one of the men opposite her say:

" 'Ere we be! Now, don' be in 'urry. We've ter get t'door opened first."

They got out of the carriage, and Nadia knew she had been left alone.

There was silence for what seemed a long time before she heard a horse shake its head, making the harness jingle and then the coachman cleared his throat.

She wondered if it would be possible to free herself from the confines of the thick blanket that covered her from her head to below her knees.

But she was afraid that if she moved, long before she could escape from the carriage the man on the box would give the alarm and the two men would come hurrying back.

They might then beat her until she was unconscious!

"I am . . . frightened! Oh, God . . . I am . . . frightened!" Nadia whispered.

Once again she cried out to Warren:

"Save me! I love you! Oh . . . save me!"

She repeated the words under her breath over and over again.

Then she thought wildly that if she were out of the way Magnolia might by some means trick him into marriage, or perhaps if he would not agree to marry her, she might hurt him in some way.

'She is ruthless and mad!' Nadia thought.

Suddenly with a constriction of her heart, she heard the two men talking together in the distance, their voices coming nearer as they approached her.

One of them pulled her out of the carriage and they both picked her up to carry her down a steep incline.

At moments, because the ground beneath their feet was rough, Nadia thought they would drop her.

Then the descent had ended and as they walked a little way on the level, one of them said:

"Moind yer 'ead!"

Nadia was sure they were stooping as if there was a low doorway above their heads, or else they were in a tunnel.

It took her by surprise when they suddenly put her down on the ground so roughly that it hurt.

And before she could get her breath she heard them walking away, their footsteps crunching on what sounded like hard, rocky ground.

In the distance a door was slammed noisily into place, a key turned in a lock, and a few minutes later Nadia could hear the sound of wheels as the carriage drove away.

It was then for the first time she moved from the place where they had thrown her down.

With an effort she eased the heavy blanket up to her shoulders, to throw it back from her head.

For one terrifying moment she thought she must have died, or gone blind, for the darkness was just the same as it had been under the blanket.

Then she was aware of a dank, damp smell and a long way from her she saw a glimmer of light.

After looking at it for some time she decided it must come from the door which the men had closed and locked.

Afraid to move, and yet realising she must find out where she was, she rose tentatively to her feet, and remembering how the men had to crouch as they carried her to where she now was, she put her hands above her head.

She touched something cold and with sharp edges.

She could just stand upright. At the same time she knew that if she moved she would be wise to bend her head.

She looked again towards the light and picking up the blanket from where it lay on the floor at her feet she walked very slowly, bending her head and feeling her way before she took each step.

The light grew stronger as she drew nearer to it, and she realised that it was coming from the sides of the door.

It was then she realised she was in a Mine. Strangely it did not smell like coal but she could not recognise what it was.

She put out her hands to touch the door and found it was very strongly made.

She pushed at it, then hammered on it with her clenched fists.

"Help! Help!"

Her voice seemed to echo back at her along the tunnel but she was sure there could be nobody outside to hear her, otherwise the men would not have brought her here.

She could feel the fear of being alone and the horror of how she would die sweep over her, and knew that unless Warren could somehow find her, Magnolia would have won.

She would die slowly of starvation, and it might be months or even years before anybody came to what she guessed now was a disused Mine.

Nadia threw the blanket with which she had been covered down onto the ground.

She sat down on it, leaning back against

the door, and covering her face with her hands she began to pray.

It was not a prayer to God, but to Warren.

"Save me!" she called to him again and again. "Save me . . . save me! I love you . . . and I do not want to . . . die before I have seen . . . you again!"

chapter seven

Outside the front door Warren found waiting the cabriolet which he used to drive round the estate and carry him to his mother's house.

Without speaking to anybody he got into the driving seat, the groom holding the horses' heads jumped in beside him and he drove off at a tremendous pace.

He knew where the Slate-Mine was, although he had not visited it for years and thought it strange that Magnolia should know of it.

He imagined she might have seen it during the hunting season when the woods and the thick stubble around the old Mine which had not been worked for years, nearly always produced a fox.

But all that really concerned him was Nadia, for he knew what had happened would shock, frighten, and distress her, so that she would quickly be in the same state of desperation that she had been in when he had first found her.

Even to think of her suffering made him feel again murderous towards Magnolia.

At the same time, he was so deeply concerned for Nadia that it was in itself a strange feeling almost like a physical pain that he had never known before.

Then as he drove on, deciding how he would comfort her and try to make her understand this would never happen again, he knew that what he had been feeling for her for a long time was love.

It seemed impossible when he had sworn to himself that never again would he humiliate himself in loving another woman after the way Magnolia had treated him.

Yet if he was honest, he had to admit that almost the moment he had met Nadia, because she was so pathetic and at the same time brave, and there seemed to be some close affinity between them which he could not put into words, he had fallen in love.

When they played their charade first to deceive *Monsieur* and *Madame* Blanc, then his mother and his relations, he had realised how exceptional she was, and how perfectly she fitted into the part he had designed for her.

Yet for Nadia it had obviously been quite natural to behave like a great lady and to be charming to his relatives.

She had moved with an indescribable grace around the great rooms at Buckwood as if she was part of them, and as he watched her something he had thought was dead within himself came to life.

At first he had not recognised it because it was so different from his initial feelings for Magnolia.

What Magnolia had awoken in him was a fiery desire, and the flame that lighted within them both was a seething, uncontrollable passion that was entirely physical.

What he felt for Nadia was spiritual and while she attracted him because of her beauty, he knew it was her mind which kept him amused, interested and intrigued.

Overriding everything else was his longing to look after her, to keep her from coming to any harm, and most of all to sweep away the fear from her eyes.

He drew in his breath sharply as he thought of how frightened she must be now.

Although she knew nothing of the Buckwood Estate, she would guess that in a place as obviously unused as the old

Slate-Mine, she could remain undiscovered for ages.

It hardly seemed possible that Magnolia should have brought into the quiet English countryside such horrors as poison and kidnapping!

Yet Warren rebuked himself for being so obtuse as not to have realised before that she was determined to have her own way almost to the point of insanity.

She had longed so desperately to be eventually the Marchioness of Buckwood, then she had lost it after it had been in her grasp, if only she had married him.

The disappointment brought out all that was fiendish and vile in her character.

"How could I have guessed, when she was so beautiful, that beneath the surface lay the heart of a devil?" he asked.

It suddenly struck him that possibly because she was so determined to be rid of Nadia she had even instructed the men who had kidnapped her to kill her before they left her in the Mine.

He knew as the thought came to him that the horror of it was like a sword piercing through him.

If he lost Nadia now he would have lost everything that was precious, so incomparable that never, however long he lived, would he find it again.

He pressed his horses to go faster in a way that surprised the groom sitting beside him.

Jim was however one of the younger lads in the stable, and Warren was glad that he would be too shy, and perhaps too stupid, to ask questions or even to think what was occurring was extraordinary.

He knew as he settled down to drive the horses that he had to travel along a rough track that led through a wood, cross a stubble field before there was another clump of trees, and beyond that the land dipped down to where the Mine had originally been excavated.

He remembered how when he was a boy his uncle had said that the slate was not worth the trouble of excavating or the cost of paying the men who worked in it.

He had therefore found them jobs elsewhere on his land, and working on the Mine had ceased.

Because it had been left neglected, the tunnels became dangerous, and before his uncle had ordered doors to be put up at the entrance in order to prevent children from playing games inside it.

It was extremely uncomfortable driving across the rough field, but Warren hardly slowed the pace of his horses.

When they passed through the clump of trees and he knew it would be easy for him to reach the Slate-Mine on foot, he brought the cabriolet to a standstill and gave the reins to the groom.

"Wait here for me, Jim," he said, and jumped down to the ground.

Then he was running, driven by a feeling of urgency which told him that if Nadia was not dead, she would be terrified at being imprisoned in the dank darkness of the Mine.

He had reached the top of the dip in the ground and saw as he expected that on the heavy doors which had been erected at the entrance there was a padlock.

For the first time he wondered if Magnolia had the key and wished he had demanded it from her.

Then he thought it more likely that the men who had imprisoned Nadia had either thrown the key away or else had taken it with them.

He hurried down the incline.

Then as he reached the doors he stood for a moment to wonder if after all Magnolia had tricked him and Nadia was somewhere else.

In a voice that did not sound like his

own he called her name:

"Nadia! Nadia!"

He thought afterwards that the few seconds he waited for her reply was a century of apprehension.

Then he heard her give a little cry before she asked:

"Warren . . . is that . . . you?"

"I am here!"

"I knew you would come . . . I have been . . . praying that . . . you would . . . save me!"

"I will do that," he answered, "but first, I have to discover how I can open the door."

He looked at the padlock and realised it was a heavy one, and it would be difficult without the right instruments to break it away from the wood.

He saw that the doors were somewhat primitively made by the estate carpenters, and merely hanging at the sides on iron hinges.

It was then that Warren knew that fate had a purpose in building up his exceptional physical strength in his long journeyings in the desert.

With a strength he knew he would not have had a year ago he put out his arms and lifted one of the doors upwards and off the hinges.

For a few seconds the strain of it seemed almost insupportable, then the door fell to the ground with a resounding crash and Nadia was standing inside.

As soon as she could see Warren's face she scrambled over the fallen door towards him, reaching out her arms so that he could lift her from the darkness of the Mine into the sunlight.

With his arms around her she knew that she was safe and that her prayers had been answered, she burst into tears.

She hid her face against his shoulder and as he held her very close against him she sobbed:

"I . . . I was so . . . f-frightened that you would not . . . know where I was . . . and that you would not . . . hear me calling for . . . you."

"I have found you," Warren said in a deep voice, "and I promise you, my darling, this will never happen again."

Because she was so surprised at the endearment she turned to look up at him, the tears running down her cheeks, her lips trembling.

Warren looked down at her and thought that despite her tears she had never looked more beautiful.

Then his lips very gently touched hers.

To Nadia it was as if the heavens opened and everything she had longed for and dreamt of and thought was impossible suddenly came true.

Warren was kissing her, and it was the most perfect, the most marvellous thing that could possibly happen.

Her lips were very soft and she trembled against him, not with fear, but with a rapture which he also felt within himself.

Because it was so perfect and so very different from any kiss he had known, his lips became more insistent, more possessive, but still he was very gentle.

He knew that he must comfort her for what she had been through, even while at the same time she entranced him.

Only when it seemed that as he kissed her time stood still did he raise his head to ask:

"My precious, my darling, you are all right? They have not hurt you?"

"Oh, Warren you are here! I was so . . . afraid you would never . . . f-find me!"

"I have found you," he said as if he must reassure himself, "and this will never happen again!"

Then he was kissing her with long, slow, possessive kisses, as if he made her his and he would never lose her.

It was a long time later when he looked down at her again and thought that no woman could look so radiant, so ecstatically, gloriously happy, and still be on earth.

"I love you!" he said again and again, as if he could not say it too often.

"I . . . love you!" Nadia replied. "But I . . . never imagined . . . never even dreamt that you might . . . love me!"

"I love you as I have never loved anybody before! And so that I can keep you safe from all these horrors which should never have happened and must never happen again, we will be married very quickly!"

It was then, to his surprise, that Nadia stiffened, and turned her face to hide it once again in his shoulder.

"What is the matter?" he asked. "I cannot believe that you do not love me enough to marry me."

"I love you with my whole heart. I love you until you fill the sky . . . the world and there is nothing else but you . . . but I cannot . . . marry you."

Warren's arms tightened around her as he asked:

"Why not?"

She did not answer, and after a moment he said:

"You must tell me your secret, my precious one, and I swear that whatever it is, nothing and nobody will prevent me from making you my wife."

"No . . . no!" she murmured. "It is . . . impossible . . . and might . . . hurt you!"

"The only thing that could really hurt me," Warren said, "is that you should not love me enough to trust me."

He felt her quiver and knew she was deeply perturbed.

"You have been through enough," he said quickly. "We will talk about it when we get home. Besides, this is not a very romantic place to be talking of our love."

Nadia raised her head and he saw she was smiling through her tears.

"Wherever we are . . . it is romantic when you tell me that you . . . love me," she said, "but . . . do you really . . . mean it?"

"I love you in a way I did not know existed until this moment," Warren said. "But come along, I refuse to stay here any longer."

He took her by the hand and helped her up the stony incline and across the rough ground of the wood to where the horses were waiting.

He lifted her into the cabriolet, picked

up the reins and Jim climbed up behind.

As they drove off, Nadia lay back against the cushioned seat feeling as if nothing mattered except that her heart was singing because she was with Warren and he had said he loved her.

Then she told herself she had to be firm, and that however much she loved him she could not let him become involved in the terror that had stalked her these last years, culminating in her mother's death.

"I have to go away and leave him," she told herself, and felt her whole body cry out at the agony of it.

Because the groom could hear what was said they did not talk, but Warren drove as quickly as he could back through the wood, into the Park and down the drive.

He did not take Nadia to his mother's house, but to Buckwood.

He did so deliberately because he felt that already she belonged there, and that was where they should decide their future.

He determined to make quite certain they would be together, and she would be his wife.

He drew up outside the stone steps, then sprang to the ground to go round to the other side of the cabriolet and lift Nadia down from it.

Then he put his arm protectively round her shoulders and led her into the house across the hall and into the Drawing-Room.

For a moment the Study was too closely associated with Magnolia for him to wish to take Nadia there.

The Drawing-Room was filled with flowers and the last rays of the evening sun coming through the windows glittered on the huge crystal chandelier.

Warren shut the door behind them and drew Nadia to one of the elegant gold-framed sofas by the fireplace.

She sat down and he said:

"My precious, you have been through so much! Shall I get you a drink?"

"I want nothing," she answered, "except to be certain that you are here and I shall not die of cold and starvation in that . . . horrible damp Mine."

She realised as she spoke that Warren was looking at her as if he had never seen her before.

"I must look terrible after having a blanket thrown over my head, and I am sure the Mine has made me very dirty."

"You look perfectly lovely!" he replied, and his voice seemed to vibrate on the word. "Lovelier than any woman I have ever seen! Oh, my darling, how lucky I was to find you!"

She knew he was referring not to saving her from the Slate-Mine, but to finding her by the Seine.

"I . . . I seem to have brought . . . you a lot of . . . trouble," she said in a low voice.

"It is all over now," he said, "but I want you to understand that the only way that you can be safe and be sure that Magnolia will never trouble us again is by becoming my wife!"

He was holding Nadia's hand, and he felt her fingers tighten on his as she said in a very low voice:

"I cannot imagine anything more . . . perfect than to be . . . married to you and to be with you . . . all the time. But because I . . . love you I cannot put you in . . . danger."

"Why should I be in any danger?"

As Warren asked the question Nadia looked away from him, and he knew she was wondering whether she should tell him the truth, or go on hiding her secret.

As he waited the door of the Drawing-Room opened and Mr. Greyshott came in.

"I heard you were back, My Lord," he said, "and thought you might like to have the newspapers which have just arrived."

He walked across the room with them in his hand and putting them down on an embroidered stool in front of the fireplace said conversationally:

"There is news that Tsar Alexander III is dangerously ill with Dropsy, and is not expected to live. You will remember your uncle visited St. Petersburg in 1882 to represent the Queen at his Coronation."

When he had put the newspapers down Mr. Greyshott looked towards Warren as if he expected an answer, and with an effort, because he found it difficult to think of anything but Nadia, he replied:

"Yes, of course, I remember!"

Then in a very strange voice that seemed as if it was spoken by a stranger Nadia said:

"D-did you . . . say . . . the . . . Tsar is not expected to . . . live?"

"That is what it says in the newspapers," Mr. Greyshott replied. "In fact, according to the *Morning Post* the doctors say his life is despaired of."

As he spoke he stared at Nadia in astonishment because she had put her hands up over her eyes, and Warren who was sitting close to her knew she was fighting for self-control.

He looked at Mr. Greyshott meaningfully, making a slight gesture as he did so, and with his usual tact his secretary understood he should leave them alone.

He walked quickly from the room, and as the door closed behind him Warren put his arms around Nadia and drew her close to him.

"I think what we have just heard means something important to you, my Precious," he said quietly.

"It . . . it means . . . that if the . . . Tsar dies . . . I am s-safe!" she said in a voice that trembled. "Oh, if only . . . Mama were still alive!"

Warren drew her closer still. Then he said:

"Tell me about it, darling. I hoped you were going to tell me anyway, before Greyshott interrupted us."

"I want to . . . you know," Nadia said. "I . . . hate having any . . . secrets from you."

"Then let us be rid of them."

She looked up at him and despite the tears in her eyes he felt in some strange way that she was suddenly transformed.

It was not only her love for him that made her face radiant, but also it seemed as if the misery he did not yet understand had slipped away from her and she was free to be herself again with all the joy and happiness of youth.

She drew a deep breath before she said:

"My real name is Princess Nadia Korzoki and my father was Prince Ivan Korzoki."

"You are Russian!" Warren exclaimed.

"Well yes, half-Russian," she confirmed. "You thought I was not . . . wholly English."

"I was sure of it," he said, "but tell me your story."

"Mama was the daughter of the British Ambassador to St. Petersburg, and Papa fell in love with her and she with him the moment they met."

She glanced up at Warren as she spoke and he knew how much she loved him, before, with an effort she went on:

"They had to have the permission of the Tsar Alexander III to marry, which he gave them only reluctantly, because Papa had Royal blood in his veins. In the end he agreed on condition that they went to live in the country on Papa's large estate which bordered on Hungary."

Nadia then paused, as if she was looking back before she went on:

"They were very, very happy, and never regretted the gaieties, or indeed, the intrigues and problems of St. Petersburg."

"So it was in Russia that you learned to ride so well!"

"I rode in Hungary also," Nadia answered, "but I have not got as far as that yet."

"Go on, my lovely darling."

"I shall always remember how happy everything was at home, but Papa was deeply shocked when Tsar Alexander II was assassinated thirteen years ago, and his son when he came to the throne revised all the reforms that were being made in the country."

Warren was listening intently as Nadia continued:

"The first thing the new Emperor did was to tear up an unsigned Manifesto which had provided for a limited form of representative Government in Russia. It was something that was very dear to Papa's heart, and it soon became clear that Alexander III was determined to bring back into Russia all the cruelties which his father had begun to eliminate."

Nadia's voice was very moving as she said almost in a whisper:

"Worst of all he was . . . determined to destroy . . . the Jews."

Warren had heard this and knew how everybody in England had disapproved of the Tsar's action.

But he did not say so, and let Nadia continue:

"The new Tsar decreed that one third of the Jews were to be exterminated, one third assimilated and one third driven out of the country."

She gave a deep sigh before she went on:

"You will understand that as Papa's estate was on the border many of those who were rounded up by the Cossacks were driven over our land, chained, starving and whipped into Western Europe!"

She fought against her tears before she went on:

"Mama used to cry at night because she had seen their suffering, and Papa helped where he could, telling our own people to give them food and sometimes, when the Cossacks were not looking, a little money."

"Then what happened?" Warren asked.

"Papa had a Jewish friend who was a very famous and brilliant surgeon, and had operated on him and on many of Papa's friends. One night he arrived at our Castle saying that he had learnt he was to be arrested the next morning and taken to St. Petersburg for investigation."

Nadia's voice was very low as she said:

"We knew this meant torture and a slow and lingering agony before he died."

"And your father saved him?"

"Papa smuggled him and his wife into Hungary and gave him enough money so that he could start life again in Europe."

Nadia made a helpless little gesture with her hands before she said:

"But of course somebody reported to the Tsar what Papa had done and he was furiously angry with him for helping such a well-known Jew to escape."

Warren began to understand what had happened.

"In fact, the Tsaravich Nicholas, who had always been very fond of Papa and was a quiet, gentle, rather weak young man, was courageous enough to send one of his trusted servants to warn Papa of the danger he was in."

"That was brave of him!" Warren exclaimed.

"Very brave, because he was frightened of his father. Anyway, as soon as Papa received the warning he hurried Mama and me to the border, knowing it was only a question of days, perhaps only hours, before he was taken to St. Petersburg."

"He did not leave with you?"

"Both Mama and I begged him to do so, but he was adamant.

" 'I will not be a Refugee from my own

221

country!' he said. 'I do not believe the Tsar would dare to execute me for a kindness to an old friend!' "

"But he did die?"

"He was . . . murdered but we did not hear about it until we were told the Tsar had commanded that Mama and I were to be brought back and stand trial also for helping the enemies of Russia, who were the Jews!"

"So that is why you were hiding!"

"We had to hide unless we wanted to . . . die like Papa."

There was a break in Nadia's voice which made Warren hold her closer to him.

"Tell me another time, if it upsets you," he said softly.

"No, no!" Nadia said. "I want to tell you . . . I have wanted to tell you before . . . but I have been too afraid to do so."

He kissed her forehead before she went on with a determination he admired:

"Everything after that became a nightmare. We had been staying with friends in Hungary, but of course we could not involve them in our troubles. Then we thought it wise to go to France, and from there to England to Mama's relatives."

"That sounds very sensible."

"That is what we thought when we

started off," Nadia answered, "but we soon realized that the Secret Police when they are intent on revenge, never give up. They tracked us all through Hungary and were not far behind us when we passed through various small Principalities until eventually we reached France."

She gave a little sob before she said:

"It is . . . difficult to remember the details . . . but it was all terrifying. All we knew was that the Russians were looking for us determined not to let us get away, and we realised that we must involve as few people as possible."

She paused for a moment before she went on:

"Nevertheless everybody was very kind, and we passed from friend to friend but as our money grew less and less we had to sell the jewels Mama had brought with her. That was dangerous because the Russians following us recognised them and knew they were only a few days behind us."

"So when you finally reached Paris you had nothing left," Warren said.

"Only the clothes we stood up in and so few francs that we could only afford to stay in an attic in a dirty, squalid lodging-house which made Mama more ill than she was already."

Nadia made a little helpless gesture as she said:

"You know the rest of the story. Mama died, and because I had nothing, really nothing . . . I wanted to . . . die too."

"Thank God I prevented you from doing that," Warren exclaimed. "But now, my precious, it is all over. The Tsaravich is your friend, and I am sure the programme of cruelty against the Jews will cease as soon as he comes to the throne."

"Do you really . . . think I am . . . safe?"

"You will be safe as my wife," Warren said, "and we are not even going to wait until the present Tsar dies. We will be married immediately, but everyone except my mother will still know you by the name we invented."

He pressed his lips against her cheeks before he went on:

"Later when it is safe to do so, we will tell the truth, and I know everybody will think it a story of great bravery, as I do."

"I, it was not very . . . brave of me to . . . want to . . . die."

"It was very brave of you to let me save you and to come here and do everything I asked of you."

She turned her face up to his and he said:

"I adore you, my beautiful little Russian Princess, and all the horrors and miseries are over. You will live a very quiet, uneventful life here in England, which perhaps after all the dramas you have been through you will find dull."

He was teasing her, but Nadia gave a little sob and put her arms round his neck to say:

"May I really do that? It sounds so wonderful, so like being in Heaven, that I feel I must be dreaming."

"It is a dream come true," Warren said, "and I assure you that when you are my wife and the Marchioness of Buckwood, there will be no Secret Police lurking in the shadows, and I will make sure there are no jealous women either."

"How can you be . . . certain of . . . that?"

Warren smiled.

He knew he had threatened Magnolia in a way which had frightened her more than he could have affected by any other means, and would ensure they were free of her in the future.

Her beautiful face was the only thing that really mattered to her and to risk damaging it for her would be unthinkable.

"She will never worry either of us again,"

he said reassuringly.

Then he had an idea.

He remembered the Special Licence with which Magnolia had tried to blackmail him.

His uncle had been a close friend of the Archbishop of Canterbury, and Warren had met him on several occasions.

He happened to know that he was in London at the moment because it had been reported that His Grace was officiating at a Memorial Service for a famous Politician who had recently died.

He was sure that if he wrote to the Archbishop asking for a Special Licence for his marriage to Nadia, and explaining that because he had just returned from abroad he was unable to come in person, the Archbishop would understand.

He could then marry Nadia immediately in the Chapel attached to the house without anybody except his mother being aware of it.

Later their marriage could be announced and their secrecy could be explained as being necessitated by his being in mourning.

Then they could entertain his relatives as he had promised them he would.

All that mattered at the moment was

that Nadia should not be left alone and frightened either by day or by night.

He felt his heart give a leap of joy at the prospect as he said:

"Leave everything to me, my lovely one. There are no more problems to be solved, no more difficulties to seem insurmountable. All you have to do is to love me."

"I do love you," she said. "I love you so much . . . but are you . . . certain you are . . . wise to marry me? After all . . . there may be some way in which it might harm you to be married to a Russian who is . . . wanted by the . . . Secret Police."

"Nothing can harm me, except that I might lose you," he replied. "What I want you to do, my adorable one, is to forget all the horrors that have pursued you from Russia, and remember that your mother was English."

He laid his cheek against hers and said:

"We will find your mother's relatives, and I know they will make you feel very much at home and a part of England. You have not been able to enjoy this country until now, but it is my country, and as we are now one person we will make it a home for ourselves and for our children."

"That is what I want to do," Nadia cried, "but I still cannot believe it is true that after so much misery and so much fear I really have come . . . home."

"I will make you sure of it," Warren said. "Oh, darling, I love you, and I swear that you will never be frightened or unhappy again."

He kissed her until the room seemed to whirl round them.

Only when Warren raised his head were they aware that the sun was sinking outside in a blaze of glory and the rooks were going to roost.

"I love you!" he said, and his voice was very deep.

"I thought you told me that you intended, if you really had to marry, to make a *mariage de convenance* as the French do!" Nadia whispered.

"I am marrying because I love you and I want you. The feelings I have for you are very different from anything I have ever known or imagined."

"What do you . . . feel?"

"Very excited — very much in love — and something more."

"What is . . . it?"

"I feel as if I have found the most precious treasure in the world which is so perfect, so unique that I will keep it and protect it for ever."

"And . . . that is . . . me?"

"You, my beautiful darling."

Warren rose from the sofa and pulled her to her feet beside him.

"I am going to take you back to my mother," he said, "and I want to tell her the truth, but nobody else. Then I am going to send my letter to the Archbishop and we will be married the day after to-morrow."

He smiled before he went on:

"Then we will leave here ostensibly to visit the other properties which I have inherited but really to spend our honeymoon together — alone."

Nadia drew in her breath and whispered:

"That will be . . . wonderful."

"We will go first to Devonshire where my house is very comfortable and very quiet and then we will go to Leicestershire to look at . . ."

Nadia gave a cry which interrupted him.

"You are doing . . . everything so quickly that I am . . . afraid."

"Of me?"

"No, I could never be afraid of you," she said, "only that you have not . . . thought it . . . over."

"I have nothing to think over," Warren replied firmly. "I am so lucky, the luckiest man in the whole world, and all that really matters, my precious, is that we are alive, we are together, and I am certainly not taking any more risks of losing you!"

He put his arms around her.

He did not say anything, but she knew he was thinking of the poison that Magnolia had tried to give her and of the men who had kidnapped her and hidden her in the Slate-Mine.

And most of all, how he had saved her as she looked down into the Seine, meaning to take one fatal step into the darkness of oblivion.

"Three times I have been . . . saved," she whispered, "and now . . . I belong to . . . you."

"I will make sure of that," Warren smiled. "Fate, or God, has given you to me, and I never dreamt it was possible to own anyone so completely adorable."

There was a passionate note in his voice which made Nadia move a little closer to him and lift her lips to his.

He looked at her before he said very softly:

"I will love you, adore you and worship you for the rest of our lives. Will that be enough?"

"It is the only thing I ever want," Nadia

whispered, "and I will love you until the world comes to an end, and the stars fall from the sky!"

Then Warren was kissing her, kissing her demandingly, passionately, at the same time tenderly, and she knew he was right.

She had 'come home.'

The employees of Thorndike Press hope you have enjoyed this Large Print book. All our Thorndike and Wheeler Large Print titles are designed for easy reading, and all our books are made to last. Other Thorndike Press Large Print books are available at your library, through selected bookstores, or directly from us.

For information about titles, please call:

(800) 223-1244

or visit our Web site at:

www.gale.com/thorndike
www.gale.com/wheeler

To share your comments, please write:

Publisher
Thorndike Press
295 Kennedy Memorial Drive
Waterville, ME   04901